ISBN-13: 9798531651433

Cover design by: Shani Clarke

D1601377

PROLOGUE

The old man lay on the wooden bed, propped on feather pillows, his breathing slow and harsh. The heavy toil of years could be read on gnarled hands and lined face.

Two young men in their late teens and two younger girls stood silently before him, their faces an anguished mixture of grief and tears. The young men wiped the tears from their cheeks, the girls did not bother, letting the wetness drip from their face. The young men were obviously twins but small differences could be discerned between them. One was slightly heavier set and a smidgen taller, but both shared the dark chestnut hair and the deep blue eyes of their sire. The girls were identical, fully grown but still carrying the bloom of youth with their flame hair and the green eyes of their mother.

The old man silently viewed his children with pride shining in his eyes and a smile on his lips. "You are all the pride of our clans. Your mother was so proud of you, she loved you so much." An audible sob was heard from one of the girls. "The three years she has been gone from us has been the hardest of my life and of yours. The wasting disease with no name was terrible for her and I'm glad she doesn't suffer any more, but I miss her more than I have words, as I know you do. She was our life, my heart. I've hung on living for as long as I could to give you all the time to grow and to learn the ways that your lives must go."

In a soft voice he went on, "People fear what they do not understand. Second Sight was her Gift from the Creator, passed down by sacred blood through long-dead ancestors of ancients Druids and Celtic Senae priestesses. As a Seer, she was fated to know an elemental wisdom and an alternate reality that was beyond her control or her desire to own. My destiny as Lord of the powerful Campbell clan was to lead with wisdom, and to protect all those under my banner. Especially the woman who was my soul's mate."

"Patrick and Peter," he held out a hand for each son to take. "You are not only my progeny, but the legacy of our clans. Your bodies have been trained as warriors to protect, and your intellect has been honed to guide in whatever form that takes. You have always known and accepted those roles, as Sword and Shield, walking in my footsteps. On your honor will you continue to do so, not only for the rest of your lives, but to pass on that knowledge to generations' future?"

Both sons dropped to one knee as a sign of their fealty, each still holding one of their father's hands. With trembling voices, they vowed, "We do so swear on our honor."

"And on mine," the old man whispered.

"Claire and Elizabeth." The young women stepped forward to stand beside a brother, both visibly holding their lips firm but tears streaming down both faces. "You know your Gifts from our Creator. Your mother taught you well. You alone have inherited and will pass those Gifts to generations' future as the Creator destines or no. Your mother and I set up as many safeguards as we could to help you. Your brothers are your best friends, and will always be by your side to assist you when choices must be made. Stay true to your birthright and pure to your mother's legacy."

Both young women knelt beside a brother, and each placed a hand on the top of a brother's hand holding their fathers, making a circle of unity. "I do so swear," both girls whispered.

The four young people knew that their mother had saved many clan leaders lives by Knowing of a plot to poison powerful leaders; Men whose names and unchangeable deeds had been permanently written on the pages of the Book of Time. In gratitude, the clans and their associates' clans had sworn their allegiance to her forevermore. They had been taught the story and it's ensuring vows throughout their childhood.

Their father had told them that he remembered the oath as

clearly today as when he and others had given it as she had stood under their circle of swords. He shared with them his own feelings of awe as a spear of white light hit his body and danced upward to the tip of his sword when he invoked the ancient rite.

As each of the other six Lords repeated the chant to invoke the ancient ritual, their touched sword tips were likewise bathed in white light. The seven swords touching each other made a mystical ring of fire, bonding ancient ancestors with their promises. The Lords, their men, and every man and woman in the castle had sworn their fealty on bended knee, sharing the oath. After all the final vows of secrecy were given, the lit swords had dimmed, and the light had disappeared.

"Remember the story of how we came to be. Please say the words of the oath with me exactly as I said them. These vows we invoke will be the power that will govern your futures and those of generations to come. Guard them well."

With tears and heartache, the four children and their father spoke the words.

"I am The Campbell. I invoke the ancient rite of Drvanetism, of those going before and those coming after. I owe my life and those of my clan to the lass beneath the circle of swords."

"Hundreds of lives have been saved by this wee lass. We invoke the spirits of the generations past and the spirits of the generations next to follow for all time to come. Let the lass and her descendant's be protected forevermore. Let her gift of Second Sight and all other gifts bestowed upon her progeny remain a Gift of her blood eternally. This we do as a rite of the old Magy and as part of our connected souls."

"In secrecy we swear to protect you and yours forevermore. We will always be your Sword and your Shield. We swear with honor."

"Let death be the judgment of any man or woman who speaks of this event of today. Today will forever be shrouded in secrecy as our own beginnings are shrouded."

CHAPTER ONE

Present Day

"**N**o, I will not!"

"Raina, be reasonable. You only have two more semesters to finish your college programs. Less than a year," Kamon coaxed, his voice raspy with control.

Raina studied the handsome man before her. Six foot one or so, slim with wide shoulder, slim hips and rigid carriage. His face was a smooth carved mask with high cheekbones revealing Native American heritage. Two thin white scars ran across his left eyebrow down to the corner of his cheek. His mid-shoulder length hair was braided into a single braid and tied with a thin strip of rawhide. Black eyes and golden complexion completed the picture of warrior status. And of the most exasperating man in her world.

"Kamon, get used to it. I am not going back. I'm twenty years old and perfectly capable of making my own decisions," Raina scowled.

"Why? Why won't you go back to school? Has something happened that I'm unaware of? Is there a reason you aren't telling me?" he demanded.

"Would you listen? No, there is no ulterior motive. The reason is just what I said, I'm spinning my wheels. Getting nowhere I want to go."

"It's just one more year," Kamon's voice was louder and angrier. "Maybe less."

"I am not going," yelled Raina in retaliation. "I. Am. Not. Damn it, you are ceaan-cath of this tribal clan but that does not make you my boss."

"No, but I am responsible for your safety. You are one of the three Ramsey women and it is my job to protect them. And stop cussing."

"Damnit, then go protect Catherine or Brenna. Oh, that's right both of them have
husbands who are trained warriors, and they don't need your protection, so all your focus can be on me," she shouted, her voice dripping with sarcasm. "And my only cuss words are damn and hell. And then only when I'm upset. Which is totally your fault."

"Their husbands take good care of them," he defended, ignoring her other comments.

"Oh, I agree with you on that issue. Trent and Deke are amazing. But that isn't the problem here. You are the problem," she declared loudly.

"I was hoping that more education would give you a direction to what you want to do".

"Kamon, listen carefully. I have done as you wanted. I majored in languages and history. I can speak more languages than anyone in the family, even Catherine. Hell, I can even speak Arabic, although why that is necessary is beyond me. I loved history, but I do not want to continue doing research. I have been the dutiful student, making exceptional grades, and doing what other people wanted me to do."

In a quieter voice, Kamon asserted, "I agree that you've been an outstanding student. That's the very reason that you should continue and graduate."

"Kamon, you are still not listening," Raina's voice was loud and inflexible. "I know what I want. I've always known, damn it. I want to stay here in Shadow Valley and help Catherine with the work of the Sgnoch Council. I want to continue hanging out with Liam and Sean, flying whatever plane they decide to modify. I want to marry and have children and …"

"All you are doing is following in Catherine's footsteps," shouted Kamon. "You don't know what you could do if you don't bury yourself here in Shadow Valley."

"You are a total idiot!" yelled Raina, not the least intimidated by the intense, angry man. "I don't need to go anywhere to find myself. I am Raina, youngest sister of Catherine, younger sister to Brenna. I am me, Raina Ramsey. And I damn well don't need to be anyone else."

"You have no experience outside the clan compounds. You've always been protected by someone from the clan," Kamon shouted.

"And whose fault is that? I've always been protected by you, or someone else you have sent to guard me. When I'm in France at the villa there, or Canada at the ranch, or in Scotland on the Island, I'm sheltered by my name, and your name as my guard. Anywhere else I go I have a Protector, a Guard you have assigned. You have no idea what's its like to have zero privacy. Zero, Kamon. Zero." She paused for breath. "Only here in Shadow Valley can I have complete freedom. And I'm damn well staying here."

"And you well know why all the Ramsey women have to be protected. And you're getting off the subject although I do admit they are tied together," admitted Kamon reluctantly. "You need experience in how the world works, and that's why it would be best continuing school where you meet other people."

"That's a crock! An absolute crock because it doesn't have a chance of working. I have an assigned guard, remember? Oh, and I live off campus with more keepers." She lifted her hand to one side pointing at an imaginary friend, "Would you like to be my new friend?" she asked in a high sing-song voice. "Oh, and this is Mr. So and So who takes every breath I do. And stays with me twenty-four seven," she continued in her high pitched falsetto. "Girl talk? Oh, he'll pretend not to listen. Oh, but we can't go to have a coffee or lunch unless he goes." She lifted her chin and stared defiantly.

A faint blush touched Kamon's high cheek bones, barely discernable with his golden skin. "It's not as bad as that," he protested softly.

"No, it's worst. My looks draw attention but I have no chance of expanding my horizons as Brenna would say. I am not, nor can I ever be a typical, normal college student."

"I am fully aware that your unusual coloring draws people's attention," Kamon said fiercely. "Everyone's attention. Mostly the male variety."

"Kamon, are you being deliberately dumb? I am isolated. By myself. I have a few acquaintances at school, but mostly other people are not interested in someone as private as I have to be. People treat me differently than the other females in any class anyway, no matter how small the class. Partially of course it's because I'm young and protected, but also because of the face the Creator gave me. Which is not my fault."

"Okay, I grant you that. How does it affect you? On a daily basis." Kamon asked curiously, his voice a shade calmer.

Raina cocked her head to the side to think through what Kamon had asked. This was the most in-depth conversation she had ever had with him. Maybe he really could listen and treat her as a grown up.

"Both teachers and other students mostly fall into two categories," she said trying to be as honest as possible. "The most prevalent is that I am brainless and can't be taken seriously. That one applies to the majority of people, including teachers, at least until the first tests. Then, of course it changes and I become some sort of nerd oddity after I ace every test. The other one is because of my coloring; the platinum hair, the blue eyes with dark brows and lashes. With my looks I'm already classified as a party-girl, and therefore I'm open season for the players on campus."

"What? Are you serious? I've never been told any of this?" Kamon said, quickly reacting with fury.

"You still don't get it," Raina said in disgust. "None of that matters. It's over. Okay, here is the bottom line. I am not going back to school. I've tried to reason with you. I've tried to be diplomatic, well as much as I can be," she corrected honestly "and nothing works. I. am. not. going. back. to. school," she said very softly, slowly enunciating each word separately.

"And you can't make me." She marched out of the room, holding her head high, and leaving a silent, frowning man behind.

Raina stomped down the stairs. Kamon was a pig-headed oaf and treated her like a pre-adolescent that he needed to boss around. Like a ten-year-old with no brains or sense. She was still not going back to school no matter what he argued. Schooling did not contribute to what she wanted for her life.

Aw, but fighting with him made her heart beat faster. Truthfully, doing anything in the presence of Kamon Young-blood brought on a flush to her skin and tingling elsewhere.

Taking a deep breath, she let it out slowly. She wouldn't tell her sister Catherine about their latest clash, the entire valley tried not to upset a newly pregnant Catherine. Her first pregnancy had been difficult with bed rest demanded before the delivery of the baby.

Catherine was the gifted tribal clan leader chosen by the clans themselves, and was thus the most important person in the valley. She alone led elders chosen from their own clans to represent them in the ancient Sgnoch Council, the decision-making group who ruled the ancient tribal clan. The Native American Scottish tribal clan buried deep in the Ozark Mountains of Arkansas in the United States.

CHAPTER TWO

"Y ou know you and Raina's battle could be heard even through the stone walls of the manor, right?" Catherine stood at the entry to Kamon's office apartment. "May I enter?" she asked.

"Of course. And I'm sorry for disturbing you. She just makes me so aggravated that I can't think rationally. She's so damn frustrating and headstrong." Kamon blew out a deep breath in exasperation.

"Kamon, have you ever talked to her? Really talked to her, like a man to a woman? And maybe even listened?"

Kamon jerked back from the window where he had been standing looking down into the courtyard below. He turned to glare at his cousin, Catherine.

"Before you lie, my friend, just remember to whom you are lying," she grinned broadly tossing her midnight gypsy-curls down her shoulder. "I am your best friend, childhood playmate, and the matriarchal leader of this tribal clan." Now her voice had dropped to a low murmur, "And you are hurting badly."

"My problem," Kamon replied sternly. "One which I will handle as I always have."

Catherine gazed steadily at her second in command, her ceann-cath. "Have you talked to her? About you?" she persisted. "Who you are? Your background before and after you came to Shadow Valley?"

"No, and I never intend to. Never," he repeated. Running a hand over his face in agitation as he repeated. "Never."

"Ah, Kamon." Catherine placed her hand on her tiny stomach bump. "Do you think it would make a difference to anyone? You were a little kid, just trying to survive."

"It doesn't lessen the fact that because of me, people died. Including my biological father. He wasn't a good man, but he was my father."

"And you didn't kill him. You were born as a Native American Mind Walker, a gift through your deceased mother's family. You didn't know that you weren't supposed to tell out loud what was in other people's minds. No one had ever taught you what you were suppose to do and not do with your abilities. And we both know the choice wasn't yours to tell, or not tell."

"Beatings do make for cooperation when you are very young," admitted Kamon wryly. "But Catherine, I'm still not going there with Raina. I can't. It would be wrong."

"Kamon, she has never made a secret of how she feels about you. She's had feelings for you since she hit puberty, maybe even before that. She adores you. She is young, yes. But she has an old soul's depth of understanding, just as Grandmother said."

"She doesn't even know me," he answered with deadly quiet. "She's just an infatuated kid trying out her new feminine wiles on what she considers a safe male. She has not the faintest idea of who I really am. And all that I have done."

"You really believe that? That she's a kid who doesn't know her own feelings? I totally disagree. Raina has always had an amazing depth to her spirit. Remember grandmother saying she was born old? She really was. She knows her own mind."

"Come on, Catherine. I'm safe, she knows I'd never do anything to hurt her. She's seen me come and go most of her life. I'm a single male, and there's not a surplus of us here in the Shadow Valley. And she's a kid."

"Twenty isn't a kid. And the other doesn't make a lot of sense. She has been in contact with other males for years at school and even here. And she hasn't expressed an interest in any of them. And Kamon, you allow very few people to know the real you," chided Catherine. "And even fewer of them get inside your thoughts and almost none into your feelings."

"Hell, if she did get to know the real me it would probably scare her to death. I'm not a very nice man and you know it. And

I never will be. I can't be, it's an impossibility. That is not my destiny."

"Not in the general sense of nice," Catherine admitted slowly. "But you are a good man in a strange kind of way, with an unusual depth of understanding and tolerance. But you're also intense, aggressive, hot-tempered, and bossy," she grinned.

"You know that I can't deny any of those assertions because not only are they all true, but you could have added a half-dozen darker claims that were equally true," Kamon grinned slightly.

"And I could have added a dictionary full of positive words that apply also," responded Catherine in a firm voice, her eyes smiling.

"Come here a moment Catherine," he asked quietly, gently holding back the curtain so they could share the view in the courtyard below.

"Look at her."

Catherine looked down at her youngest sister.

Raina was picking up toys strewn in the courtyard by the valley's children who often played within the sheltered spot. Her stick straight hair hung to her waist and was a cross between platinum and pale liquid gold. Dark lashes and brows, oval face and if he could have seen her downcast eyes, he knew they would be crystal blue.

He sighed, "She is everything I'm not. She's young, and I'm so jaded that I feel a hundred years old. She's an innocent, and I've done things during the wars and afterward that scares the living hell out of me looking back at them. I've seen too much, Catherine. Felt too much. And frankly, I've been too much. I know that my own personality is so intense and so complicated that I overwhelm others when I let myself go. Control has to be my mantra. It's better this way."

He let the drapes fall back into place to face his clan leader. "You do know that I'm a freak of nature. A throw-back. There hasn't been a documented Mind Walker for five generations. Grandfather Youngblood thought that Mind-Walking is a remnant of the long ago Native American Skin-Walker, that shapeshifter rumored throughout many native cultures. And most native peoples throughout the world have histories in which he was involved in some way. He could be either evil or good. So, what does that make me?"

"Right now, it pretty much makes you a total idiot," declared Catherine flatly, pushing her jet curls away from her face in agitation. "You are what you are. You didn't choose. None of us did. Remember mine and Brenna's t-shirts that said 'The Creator does not make mistakes'? Well, that's us. We were born as we are, with special attributes or not. And Raina's only skill is her inability to lie. She doesn't have a unique gift. She told me the other day that she's never been jealous that Brenna and I have unusual gifts as a Seer and Healer. Raina is happy in her own skin."

"Because everyone loves her. She loves easily. There isn't one person in Shadow Valley that isn't her best friend. Just being around her raises everyone's spirits. And me? I'm moody and most of the time difficult on my best days. I like so few people that I could count them on one hand almost."

"I'm glad you are as you are. Without you my life's work would be more difficult."

"And It doesn't make me any more right for her no matter how either you or I feel. I'm too old, too experienced, and ugly inside. Really ugly inside. For once Catherine, you really can't understand. I'm not worthy to love her. All I can do is to protect and keep her safe. Sharing her life? I would hurt her in so many ways that it would kill my very being."

"But Kamon ...," Catherine started to respond.

"I'm too different. And yes, I am aware that a few people in Shadow Valley are different, but look around you, Catherine, I try to keep my office here as austere as possible to cut down on stimuli, much like you do. When I have to make hard decisions, it's easier for me if I'm not in comfortable surroundings."

He waved a hand toward his large scarred desk, bookcases so full that the excess was stacked neatly on the floor. Deep brown leather sofas and chairs completed the room's furnishings. Only the two pictures on the wall held any color, a framed picture of Grandfather Youngblood as a young man, and another picture of the three Ramsey women taken about three years before.

"I grant that your office is less messy than mine," she grimaced. "But in reality, putting your world in cubbyholes is sometimes necessary to focus when a problem arises. I know that I have to separate my work from my family, and sometimes the Sgnoch Council. It's normal for people with unconventional attributes like us. You have the strong will necessary to do the part that a tribal clan leader needs, and the fortitude to carry out those responsibilities."

Catherine paused, then continued, "But there's another part of you Kamon that you hide from most people. You are respectful with Mother Earth. It especially shows with your architecture designs of homes here, blending them into nature. None of which has anything to do with your private life and your emotions."

"Thank you for your kind words. I love to design and remodel structures, and I'm consistently humbled by the experience. And I'm going to ignore all your previous remarks about Raina." He gave a derisive snort. "Catherine, I'm glad to serve you and the clans. The ancestors actually set up a good system when they proclaimed that if the chosen leader was a female or young, they could choose a second in command, a ceann-cath, a warrior for the physical safety of the clan."

"It was part of the Native American matrilineal ideology and the Scots long-time history. When the Scots intermarried into the Native Americans communities, that is one of the philosophies of both of their belief systems."

"And a very smart one for both cultures. We both know that women often live longer than warrior men so a matrilineal matriarchal line where women inherit makes better sense. For me, I don't know what I would have done with my life if you hadn't asked me to serve, and truly needed me as your second in command."

"You would have done something equally important, but

I'm glad to have my friend near as my advisor and ceann-cath. Now back to Raina, what was the yelling about?"

"She says she's not going back to school. That she's staying here in the valley. Her immediate plans are to help you, and I quote 'hang out with the twins'." He ran long slim fingers over the side of his hair smoothing unseen strands into the leather strip holding back his long black hair. He had recently adopted the longer hair and braid for convenience.

Catherine spoke slowly, "The consequences of Raina remaining in Shadow Valley would certainly change things. In one way, she would be a tremendous help to me. She has the ability to organize a small country, and she can focus completely on a problem. She speaks a multitude of languages, and listens with her heart. For you however, having her here would be a lesson in frustration, right? She's an independent spirit and doesn't take well to being bossed, which you still seem to want to do with her. And she would be a part of your everyday life."

Kamon gave a quick nod, reining in his temper. Self-control was primary.

"For her, she needs more experience in the outside world. She has been too protected and hasn't had to learn the hard lessons, or to make decisions without a back-up. I envy her that she can travel," Catherine declared with a slight grimace.

Kamon smiled sympathetically at his best friend, recognizing the truth in her words. Catherine had been given the gift of Second Sight before birth. Her time outside the valley was limited as the strength and number of stimuli overwhelmed her senses. She needed peace, quiet, and harmony in order to exist, without it she became physically ill. Catherine was from a long line of Ramsey women following the strict edits laid down by the Ancient Ones.

Their history, and the histories of Shadow Valley, were the story of the girl-woman ancestor with Second Sight who had lived in the middle 1700's. She had saved the lives of clan Lords and their followers from mass poisoning; the leaders and their progeny whose future existence and deeds had already been written in the Book of Time. She had been rewarded with the protection for her future generations and any Gifts the Creator bestowed on them.

With the Gift of Knowing, the girl-woman had seen the coming massacre at Culloden where the English had brought Scotland to her knees and forever changed the clans and their way of life. She had also Seen the turmoil and potential death of many Scots through starvation and deprivation.

She had advised her children and those others who chose to join them, to move to the new country of the Americas. There they could carve out a hidden valley where they would be able to live with both freedom and peace. And to be able to keep their Gifts without reprisal from man, and man's made-up laws.

The group had sailed for the small port of New Orleans and then journeyed up the mighty Mississippi River to the White River, then on to its river tributaries. Then the group had trudged up a mountain range to one of the most rugged parts of the Ozark Mountains to a small valley where they settled a community in the forested rocky terrain. An area in what would many years later became part of the state of Arkansas.

Only a handful of trappers had ever ventured into the Ozarks at that early time. Native Americans had lived in the local cliffs and forests for hundreds of years however. The Osage, and later the Cherokee and Choctaw mixed freely with the new arrivals as the Scottish people had always married into the local populations wherever they traveled. As they intermingled tribes and clans, both groups were forever changed into one.

"Are you okay, Kamon? You looked lost there for several minutes."

"Actually, I was thinking about when our ancestors first came here from Scotland and the Native Americans who were here. The conditions must have been unbelievably primitive and difficult to survive."

"Their journals speak of hardships but also a sense of freedom, of becoming and evolving into who we are. Striving to keep the best of what each clan system was, and intermingling it

15

with our Native American cultures as we mixed our blood. And again, we have strayed from the subject. Raina."

"I actually wasn't straying from it; I was avoiding it. She's so frustrating that she makes my teeth ache." Taking a deep breath, he added, "I think I need to get away for awhile. Relieve some of my tension so I can live to fight another day," he grinned ruefully. "And before you ask again, no. I will never go there. Never. She isn't for me. I cannot ever allow myself to love her. I can only protect her."

Catherine gave a deep sigh as she walked out of Kamon's office suite.

Sean McKinney, a cousin, grinned at her from the bottom of the stairs. "Hey, Catherine. I'm looking for Raina. We're going to go over that new engine prototype from Lockheed in a couple of hours, and I promised Raina that she could be there. Liam's flying in from Exeter with supplies. Of course he might be late seeing as his girlfriend is now working there." He chuckled in good humor adding, "Don't blame him a bit."

He was quiet for a moment, searching Catherine's dismayed appearing face. "Is anything wrong?"

"Not something any of us can do anything about," she clarified. "Anyway, Raina was in the courtyard a few minutes ago, but if she isn't there, try the library. She said this morning that she wanted to check one of the older journals for information on Grandmother's aunt."

"Didn't know she had one."

"Apparently a lost one. It looks like she ran away when she was just a girl. I haven't been able to pick up anything on her. Of course I would not be able to See her since she is close in blood."

"Okay, I'll try the library first."

Catherine watched as Sean walked away. Why Raina wasn't chosen as a mate for Sean was a mystery she would never unravel. Sean with his mathematical abilities and easy-to-get-along-with persona would be ideal for anyone. Unfortunately, Raina was laser focused on Kamon Youngblood and had been forever. Catherine had to admit there was a strong magnetism between the two, at least on Raina's part.

"Destiny." She murmured softly to herself. "Destiny."

"Hey Raina," Sean greeted as he spied her on the second floor of the massive library. Built of mahogany, bookcases lined the first-floor walls, interspersed with tables, leather sofas and plush chairs sitting on Persian carpets. Light poured in from tall beveled windows with curtained window seats beneath. Above the huge brick fireplace was a large picture frame displaying an old Bow and arrow. A faded Ramsey tartan of red and black with a thin line of white running through the plaid was arranged across the bow.

A winding staircase led to an upper floor circling the downstairs. Mahogany rails enclosed the entire level holding small tables and chairs. Floor to ceiling bookcases with older-looking tomes were housed on the second level. Raina was kneeling, looking through a small glass bookcase with old bound books inside.

"Liam will be back from Exeter whenever he can tear himself away from Beth, and we're going to go over the new engine from Lockheed. Liam thinks that with a little modification we can reduce the fuel consumption even more and be safer. Want'a go?"

Raina put back the small old books and carefully closed the beveled glass cabinet housing them. "Absolutely. I'm there," she declared with a wide grin. "I'm trying to find references to Grandmother's aunt, but I've not found much."

"You love that kind of stuff," he shrugged showing his lack of interest. "Hey, I just ran into Catherine and she looked, I don't know, not upset exactly but something not quite right."

"Damn, she probably heard Kamon and I shouting at each other," she groaned. "I told him I was not going back to school. Period. Not next semester. Not ever. I'm done with school. You're right, I love the learning but not the slow-moving classes."

"Ugh. I'm glad I wasn't in on that battle. Kamon is too much a warrior for me. Cousin or no, he could eat me for lunch."

"Well, not me. Nope, not me. He'd never hurt me. He just likes to boss and wants his own way."

CHAPTER THREE

"**N**o, please no. Please, please, no," she begged.

Sean turned his head to see Raina looking out the car window with horror and disbelief on her face. He leaned forward in his seat trying to see what had upset her and caused her horrified reaction.

Kamon Youngblood. It would have been impossible to mistake the six foot plus dark-haired man. He was standing on the porch of a white clapboard house, his arm around a young woman, her glowing face tipped toward his. She pulled him into an embrace and then kissed him, slowly and thoroughly. Then he took her hand and led her inside the small house shutting the door quietly behind him, never noting the car that had observed him from the street.

"Sean, stop. I can't breathe." Raina's breath was coming in short burst of air as she fought to stay in control. "No, oh no."

"Can't stop now. Let's get out of this neighborhood first. The last thing we need is for Kamon to think we were spying on him," he argued tightly, stepping harder on the car's accelerator.

A few minutes later, Sean pulled the car into a sparsely occupied grocery store parking lot. "This will give us some privacy. Raina, I don't know what to say. You're my closest female friend. I wish I knew how to help you but all my brain does is come up with platitudes which you don't need."

"Please, Sean, don't say anything else." Raina took deep breaths, panting. "Ah, damn. That hurts so bad. So bad." Tears rolled down her face as she rocked back and forth trying to find her own comfort. "Ah damn." She shuddered as if cold.

Sean put his arm around her and pulled her against his chest, saying nothing. Her tears fell silently for several minutes, and then her shudders became less and less as the shock wore off. Sean's shirt was soaked with salty tears by the time she got herself into a semblance of control.

"I didn't know. I didn't know there was someone else. How could I not know? How could I not see?" Her voice shook as she closed her eyes to hold back tears which still leaked beneath her lashes. "I shouldn't have fought with him this morning. I should have...," she bit off the rest of her sentence.

Sean remained silent.

"Who is she? Do you know her? Why didn't someone tell me?" Raina continued to hug herself and rock back and forth. "Oh God, Sean. My insides are crushed. I've loved him since I was twelve years old. Since he came back to visit with Grandfather Youngblood. He's everything I always wanted. Why Sean? Why?"

"For starters, I don't think anyone knows of this relationship. Liam and I certainly didn't," he said referring to his identical twin. "There have been rumors of various liaisons over the years but nothing concrete so you weren't ever told. There was nothing to tell," he shrugged. "Besides what would you have done? And as to who she is, I've never seen her before."

"Oh my God. I hurt. Does Catherine or Brenna know do you think? Why? Why wasn't I ...," her voice trailed off, not wanting to think of the implications of her sisters hiding secrets from her. Being ten years younger left her out of some of their conversations however.

"No, I don't think anyone knows. Catherine would be blocked by her close relationship with Kamon to have any idea. She may have guessed, or Trent may have told her something, but she would not have any Sightings of Kamon. Brenna and Deke are working that disaster site in Oklahoma and I have no idea how much, or if they know anything about Kamon's private life. And Kamon is extremely tight-lipped and private, as you well know. He doesn't talk about himself."

"Ah Sean. I feel sick. I need to vomit." Tears seeped under her lashes and rolled onto her cheeks but she quickly swiped them away. "My entire being has been focused on a relationship with Kamon. Everything I am. My God, the years I've given him in my heart. Every thought, all the love I had growing up. I never thought of a relationship with anyone else. I never looked at anyone else as a possible mate. I thought he was destined for me. I hate him. I really hate him. I feel destroyed."

She thought back to all her teasing and innocent flirting. How she had virtually opened her heart to him. She had never seriously considered any other man as a mate, only Kamon with his long black hair and dark fathomless eyes. She had thought he was the most handsome being in the universe. Now she just felt sick to her stomach.

"Raina, I could try to beat the shit out of him for you, but he would probably kill me."

"He wouldn't care enough about me to bother," she said bitterly. "My youthful dreams. He probably laughed his head off when I told him that he was only for me. That we were destined to be together. Ha, that's a laugh." She held her hands tightly over her mouth to stop the trembling.

Head bowed she whispered, "Now what? What in the hell am I going to do?"

"If you're really asking, well the truth is that I don't know. Most of the family expected a mating between you and Kamon eventually. It's what you wanted and he was always very, very protective of you." He shrugged his shoulders, "I don't know what to say to help you. I've never felt that way about anyone. Liam does about Beth Gowan. So far all that has eluded me, thank you." He glanced upward in tribute.

"I don't want to see Kamon again. At least not now. Maybe never. I need to just disappear." Biting her lower lip, she continued, "I can't see him again. I can't, Sean. It would be more painful than even I could take. Knowing that he and that woman…." Fresh tears streamed down her face unchecked as she asked her best male friend, "Will you help me?"

"Of course," he answered immediately. "Whatever you need, you know I'll help. But Raina, you're going to have to have a plan, and you have to get permission from Catherine to do whatever you're thinking of doing. You're still Raina Ramsey. You have duties and responsibilities just like I do."

"I know but …. I can't pretend that everything is the same. It isn't. I'm not. As young Maggie would say, this has knocked the stuffing out of me. Changed how I feel inside."

She swallowed hard, and then straightened up in the seat. "Maybe this is meant to be. What do Catherine and Brenna always say? Destiny wills. I can't go back though, at least not for awhile. I'm not good at pretending, I never have been. And I refuse to act as if everything is the same. When it damn well isn't."

"No. It's not," agreed Sean. "You're honest and too straight-forward for your own good, but not going back to Shadow Valley is out of the question. You have to go back and you know it. And I know it. You have to discuss whatever you plan to do with Catherine. Only she can give you permission to whatever you need to do."

At her frowning glare, he went on, "Come on, Raina, you're the planner extraordinaire. You can do this. For years you've planned and organized everything in the valley and some things that aren't. Think of this in a linear fashion, like it was someone else's problem. Now, you don't want to see Kamon right now, correct?

"Right, I just can't," Raina's voice trembled with emotion. "I really will not able to look at him and to know that woman has a part of him I've never seen, no puns intended. I know there was no understanding between us, but I thought he was mine. Mine. That he would be my permanent joining with a shared life and children. What was intended for me this lifetime."

Ignoring Raina's outburst Sean continued, "Two, you're going to need someone to go with you wherever you decide to go. You are the last unmarried Ramsey female direct descendent from the girl-woman. You know the rule. If Catherine, Brenna, or you go out of the valley or the other properties you have to have a Protector with you. Especially you. You're the last single Ramsey woman. Whoever mates with you first, by force or not, you are bonded to for the rest of your life. And you will need a Protector that has been approved by the Sgnoch Council and Catherine, of course."

He looked sternly at the tear-stained face. "Now, I am willing to fulfill that bodyguard protection role for you as long as it's needed."

He held up his hand in the stop position as she started to interrupt. "Actually, that was supposed to be either mine or Liam's assignment anyway after we went through the Warrior Society training, but Kamon decided to fulfill that role himself. As ceann-cath of the clan he has that right with Catherine's permission, of course."

"True. I thought it was because he cared for me. That he wanted to protect me himself. Wanted to be sure I was safe. So much for that fantasy," she snorted as she leaned back against the headrest letting her platinum hair fall forward across her breast and onto her waist.

Again ignoring her, he added, "Three, we have to involve Catherine after you decide what you want to do. I would suggest you decide to do something that we have an outside chance of getting approved before we talk to her. She is going to insist that wherever you go, it must be safe. Do you want to go back to school?"

"Absolutely not. I like the learning part, but as I told you I'm done with the school part." Raina was gaining a modicum of control by breathing deeply in and out. "I'll have to tell Catherine the truth, no matter what. I feel she has to know what I saw. And I need my big sister's support, probably both my sisters backing. I've had my head in the sand for so long that it's difficult to think of alternatives. You'll go with me to see Catherine?"

"Of course. We're going to have to stick together if we have any chance at all of getting Catherine's permission. Now, you've always been able to organize anything and everything. The tribal clan has always said that you could organize a small country. Now organize two people out of an area that they need to leave. Really, in one sense, it will not be a hardship for me to go wherever you want to go for awhile. Liam has Beth, and I'm glad for him, but Liam is not me. Identical bodies and faces, but inside you know how different we really are."

"I do and I'm grateful for you, Sean. Crap, why couldn't it have been you and me?"

"No chemistry between us for either of us. For years you've treated both me and Liam like not-too-bright brothers that you could boss, manipulate and generally act as a bratty younger sister. Both Liam and I have loved being a part of a threesome that share so many aspects of our lives. You're a brat and we love you, but you and I don't have those special feelings toward each other. I love you like my sister, but frankly, no thanks. I want someone simpler in my life. We're too different, and you're too pretty. Besides you're too blasted bossy."

"Thanks ijit," she said affectionately sniffing back the tears. "I could think better with my head if my heart didn't hurt so much." She closed her eyes and tried to empty her mind and relax. She took several deep calming breaths. "If I was organizing a trip that Catherine would approve of, it would either be to one of the other places we have like the Island in Scotland, or one of the other residences. Or we could go to a relative, say Marie in Paris who would be glad for help with the children. But I don't want to do any of those things. It would still be part of our life and of Kamon's. We wouldn't have accomplished anything. My situation would be the same, just in another location."

"Well, another option would be to go out of country and work, say in the International Aid organization. I'm sure we could get Brenna's old boss to let us do some volunteering somewhere," Sean suggested.

"That's true. Another idea would be to simply go and help Brenna and Deke in Oklahoma with tornado disaster relief," added Raina warming up to the idea. "The town of Parker was hit hard with almost half the town either destroyed or in need of repair. They're going to be there for at least another week or so. Afterward we can make the decision of what's next. I'm sure Brenna and Deke wouldn't mind us helping out," she paused, frowning in concentration. "I think I like that best. What do you

24

think?"

Brenna Ramsey, Raina's older sister, had married Deke Paxton more than two years before. They had a little boy, Brandon, and Brenna was in the very early stage of a new pregnancy. Since their marriage, they had worked as a volunteer team in disaster places that needed their unique skills.

"I like it. You would have another sister to talk with, and Deke could show me how I could help. And we can probably get Catherine's permission with Brenna and Deke already there. We do need to have her help in a lot of ways. Running away is going to take a lot of effort to do it right. Let's get to the airport. I'll fly the chopper back."

"The sooner we can talk to Catherine the better."

At the large modern airport, Sean drove along the tarmac to a building located just behind the executive airplane section. Pilots new to the area were startled at the large modern airport in the small-town setting. They were told that a giant department store company used it for regional storage services. A half-truth. The airport had been expanded by Glen Gowan, owner of an international big-box company, under the guise of needing more space for a regional transport center, which was true.

A section of the airport was set aside for the exclusive use of private jets. What was generally not known was that behind that area were several large hangers and a couple of runways for the sole use of airplanes and helicopters from Shadow Valley. The area was as restricted as possible without drawing attention.

The young man who worked at the back airport hangers greeted Sean, and helped pull the little helicopter onto the deserted tarmac built away from the general flow of planes. He thanked the attendant, quickly went through the pre-flight check-off list, and climbed into the pilot's seat.   Flying was the normal mode of transportation for the isolated valley called Shadow Valley built into the side of Sky Mountain deep in the Ozark Mountains of Arkansas. The public road leading to the isolated property was poorly maintained on purpose, keeping automobile traffic to a minimum.

With the advice of their gifted leader with Second Sight, the ancient ancestors had chosen well for their home. The tall mountains of the Ozarks shielded the green valley from harsh winter weather so prevalent to the area. A warm wind current of a banana belt at the base of the mountain range kept the temperature more moderate and allowed a thick grove of trees to thrive. Crops and edibles also flourished, which in the early days were essential to survival of the small immigrant group. Each generation added to the valley's isolated sustainability, and constantly monitored the secrecy.

From the air Shadow Valley looked like a tipped shallow bowl with tall canopied trees and thick green forests. Hues of green stretched out as far as the eyes could see. Massive oak trees acted as umbrellas to shelter roads within the valley and mix with smaller trees of pine, ash, and fir. New technology built into the brown or green-colored road base helped liquefy the snowfall, making roads within the valley usable year-round. From the sky the entire mountain range, including Shadow Valley, looked like an impenetrable green mass of trees, shrubs, bushes and clinging vines.

The small Sanhicks Airport was Shadow Valley's airport built into Sky Mountain's hillside. It was a technological wonder and brainchild of Jonathan Hicks, who was born and died in Raina's great grandmother's generation. He had served in the Second World War as a pilot in a B-17, the Flying Fortresses, and loved flying. After he returned from the war, he had carved out a dirt runway from the side of the mountain to make a landing strip for his small private airplane. The availability of air travel made the remote isolated valley more assessable to needed services and easier to live within.

Unfortunately, it also made the valley and its air strip more visible from the sky, and possible detection from the outside world.

Grandmother Ramsey, with her wide range of technological resources, had solved the problem temporally by cutting deeper into the side of the mountain. Scottish engineers had used Mother Nature's trees and forests for camouflage along with strategically placed boulders.

Raina's sister, Catherine, with her gifted penchant for electronic gadgetry added her share along with the McKinney twins' genius for modifying machinery. With help from their German engineering friends, together they solved the problem of hiding an entire airport. Liam and Sean McKinney lived most of the year in the valley, and used the Sanhicks Airport as their mechanical lab base.

"It's always a thrill to watch when the sensors pick up our DNA," Sean commented to Raina, as he flew over a large tree strewn meadow. "I know I'm home."

"Yeah," Raina agreed in a soft voice.

Immediately the meadow began to change. What had minutes before been a small rock-strewn meadow with gigantic oak, elm, and short-leaf pine trees was now moving to one side of the area. The intermittent trees and large man-made stones had slid smoothly back several hundred feet to display a green grassy-looking airport tarmac. Trees and rocks sat side by side at the edge of the meadow along with several bush-like trees of sassafras and pine, all waiting to be moved back onto the meadow mechanically.

Raina knew the materials had been initially developed by DuPont for use in outdoor carpets, but Liam and Sean had altered the formula slightly to produce the unique green asphalt. The trees and shrubs were straight out of Disneyland. In fact, the landscape designer of Sanhicks had been one of the people who had built the fantasy world, although he thought it was for a to be constructed theme park. From the air it was impossible to differentiate the hundreds-old trees from their manufactured fakes.

Liam and Sean insisted the entire setup was nothing more than fancy conveyor belts using electronic sensors, communicational physics interfaced with computer vision, and tied to an electronic satellite system. Raina rolled her eyes every time the twins tried to explain the dynamics to her. To her, it made more sense to think of the landscape as fancy green conveyor belts.

All the residents of Shadow Valley kept up a guessing game of which trees were real and which were authentic imitations. It had become a favorite sport especially among the older residents. Raina always thought they didn't have enough to occupy their time.

Only on landing were green Quonset-type airplane hangers seen carved into the mountain and covered on three sides by Ozark dirt and grass. Several men could be seen working through one of the open doors.

Shadow Valley was a small part of thousands of acres of mountain land, given to the Ramsey clan in the mid-1700's from the French King, and then upheld by President Jefferson during the Louisiana Purchase. All the acreage was electronically fenced and visually monitored by satellite, with a large part of it as a wild life preserve.

After two hundred fifty years, it still remained isolated and secretive. The home of Clan Ramsey and its associates.

CHAPTER FOUR

C atherine slowly laid down her pen. "You two wanted to see me immediately. Mrs. Searle said it was important. I know you wouldn't interrupt me if it wasn't, sweetie. And you've been crying, Raina. How can I help?"

Catherine Ramsey was sitting at a small desk in an alcove outside her communication center. She was a petite woman with jet black messy curls, dark eyes, and a clear creamy complexion. And she was in the first trimester of pregnancy with a tiny baby bump.

The door to the center where she had been working was open. The walls back of her held a multitude of computer-like screens, most of them active and showing everything from numbers from the stock exchanges throughout the world to a satellite picture of Russian oilfields. On the desk was a computer-like device holding an assortment of unique-looking application icons. On several tables in another alcove were more unrecognizable machines and devices.

"I'm sorry to interrupt Catherine but I really need you." Raina bit her under lip to keep control of her tears. "There's no easy way to say this so I'll tell you what we saw." She took a deep breath.

"Sean and I took the little helicopter down to Spring Creek to pick up those syringes that Brenna ordered for Shadow Valley's clinic. We were also checking out oil consumption for a new airplane fuel Liam and Sean are modifying."

She took another deep breath, blowing it out slowly. "We were driving through that older section of town, taking a short cut back to the airport. Anyway, we saw Kamon there. He was standing on the front porch of this house. There was a woman with him, smiling into his face. He embraced her, and then she kissed him. A real slow kiss like she had done it a hundred times before. Not a peck on the cheek."

She closed her eyes for a moment to regain control. Tears seeped under her lashes. "He took her hand, pulled her close against him, and they went into the house. He had his arm around her waist and she was leaning into him."

Raina struggled to hold back her emotions, making her voice as steady as she could. "Catherine, I've always thought of him as my someday mate, my permanent joining. He has been everything to me. I only wanted him. I could see no other. There wasn't a day that went by that he wasn't in my thoughts. Since I was twelve."

Catherine remained silent. Waiting.

"To say my world is shattered is an understatement. My very practical self is heartbroken, disappointed and confused," she gulped trying to stay in control as she fought back tears.

"Sean?" asked Catherine.

"It's as Raina says. We saw Kamon with a woman in an intimate-looking situation. They kissed, and then he took her into the house."

Taking a deep breath, he stated, "Before Raina goes any further with her wishes, I want to formally petition you, and through you the Sgnoch Council, to become Raina's Protector. Raina and I have talked about it and she agrees that it would be best, at least for now. Liam and I have been trained by the Warrior Society and you know that I would guard her with my life."

"I don't doubt that, Sean. That's some serious consideration. Again, Raina, how can I help?"

Nibbling on her lower lip Raina replied, "I need to go away for awhile. I need for my heart to heal, to adapt to what is now, not what I want it to be." She added with only a small break in her voice, "What it can never be for me again. What did Grandfather Youngblood say, "The world only turns one way and we really can't move the clock backward? I know that and what I saw changes everything for me. Forever."

Catherine listened silently, her face filled with sadness.

"Catherine, I wasn't enough. Old enough, wise enough. Enough of whatever he needed. What he wanted. I thought that it was only a matter of time before he looked at me as a mate. He knew how I felt, but I was fooling myself. I thought he was waiting for me to grow up. I guess now I start that process. Now I need time to learn that my intimate world does not include Kamon Youngblood."

"I understand what you are saying Raina. Are you sure you don't want to talk to Kamon about what you saw? Maybe there's an explanation."

"Good grief, no. Absolutely not! And Catherine, I'm neither stupid nor naive. I know all the implications of what we saw. Kamon has a relationship with the woman, one of intimacy. And one that didn't develop today. Whether it's his fault or my own, I hate him right now for taking away my dreams, childish ones or no. Right now all I want to do is to kill him or at least do him great physical harm like cutting him into tiny pieces. And I feel crushed," she added her eyes brimming with tears.

"Raina, I do know that you're neither stupid nor naive," Catherine stated in her calm, soothing voice. "You have been able to live outside the valley your whole life whenever you've wanted, although that hasn't been often because you've chosen to stay here. You've been educated as normally as it was possible under our circumstances. But you do know that for a normal man or woman to have a physical relation is not the same as it is for the three of us. A sexual liaison, for want of a better word, may not affect a man's or a woman's heart. It may mean next to nothing, a physical release for Kamon."

"I do know that men and women can have meaningless sex, but the way Kamon held her was like he really cared. Oh Catherine, you should have seen him. He held her gently like she was precious to him. Not at all like the tough warrior he normally is." Raina's tears reappeared in her eyes. "I need to get away to regroup. To decide where I want to go from here."

"I'm so sorry this happened, Raina. Your heart must hurt dreadfully. I know that Trent had other ladies before me but I still hate the idea. To see one…, it must be so painful. I can understand your need to get away for now."

Raina stood silently waiting for Catherine's decree. Catherine alone ruled the tribal clan and whatever she dictated it would be carried out. Without question.

"O-kay," Catherine spoke slowly drawing the word into two syllables, "that makes sense. You are the planner of our valley and you have been well trained. Obviously, you have a proposal for what you want to do for now. Or at least some ideas."

"Sean and I discussed lots of ideas but the best one we think is to help someone else, to get beyond ourselves to gain a new perspective. To learn about other people and maybe be of some assistance to them. That's something that neither of us has ever had a chance to do."

"That sounds so much like Grandfather Youngblood's teachings. That makes him proud."

Grandfather Youngblood had died almost three years before but his thoughts, ethics and moral principals were ingrained into the three Ramsey women and in many others. He had often told them that nothing was lost, not even through death. People simply crossed into the Valley of Beyond where the veil between the worlds is thin and made of mist.

"We talked about several options, but we were thinking of joining Brenna and Deke in Oklahoma in their disaster relief. Sean and I both know first aid and I know a little of other basic EMT stuff. Sean is a certified EMT. Neither of us are afraid of hard work and can do clean up too. Maybe they could use a little help with Brandon. An almost two-year-old can be exhausting. I remember when Maggie and Douglas were that age."

"Good grief, I sincerely hope Brandon never has their kind of energy," Catherine shuddered. "Those two have to be unique, there can't possible be two more of them in the world. They don't try to attract trouble but mischief follows them wherever they go." She blew out a huff of breath.

"Back to you, Raina. I'm going to give you my permission for two reasons. First, I can understand your need to recover away from here. To take a breather as you will. You've been hurt and need to heal. And healing will be easier if you are away from Kamon where you don't have to see him every day."

"Second, you do need to live outside the tribal clan's borders for more experience and to just see what other people in the world see. Where you can grow and become whatever is you. We have the tendency to smother you in our habit of protection, especially Kamon and I."

Catherine turned to Sean, "Are you sure you want to leave the valley right now? You have projects in the works with Liam. Liam could probably do much of it by himself, but you must be absolutely sure what you are asking. You know that if you take the assignment you must stay with Raina at all times until she no longer has the need, or someone else has been trained for her. That will limit your future plans, making it virtually impossible for you to work here with Liam if Raina isn't here too. You do understand that, right? Wherever she goes, you go also."

"Yes, I do realize that the assignment is almost permanent and I take that very seriously, but I too need to get away, Catherine. We've all talked about being born twins as a double-edged sword. It's wonderful in so many ways to be half of something, but it also has its drawbacks. For Liam and me we are not only identical in looks, but have been blessed with almost identical minds. Thankfully, our personalities are very different, and I want to be on my own for awhile. To not have Liam to depend on. To be separate. Being half of anything isn't whole, it's still half. Does that make sense?"

"Yes, it does. Have you discussed this with him?"

"No, of course not," Sean's voice showed his shock at the idea. "Your permission is first."

"I have one major stipulation before I give an affirmative. Wherever you travel, volunteer to work among the local population for at least a week, but preferably longer. I don't care what you volunteer for, but it must be a need that you can meet. This is not essentially a sight seeing trip, but one in which you learn. And by interacting with the local population you will have that opportunity. Do you understand?"

"Yes, of course," answered Raina as she looked at Sean. "We must find something in every locality where we can help, then spend at least a week working there to gain a different perspective or viewpoint."

"Right. Sean, then when Raina goes, you have my permission to be her Protector and of course, I will deal with Kamon. I will also talk to Liam and the Sgnoch Council. No details will be given as Kamon is part of the Council. Please do not use your own names for anything. Use the names of Shane and Anna Donovan, ancestors from long ago. We will need to protect you both from speculation not only as you travel, but within the clans."

She was silent for a moment then continued, "We will leave your return date flexible, just let me know once a week how you both are. It would be best if where you go is a secret known only to me. I will simply say I have given permission for the two of you to go awanderin' as our ancestors have done for eons. No one will question my decision."

"Awanderin', going where the breeze blows. Grandfather always said that."

"Yes, he did. Be sure to take enough money. The attainment of money has never been a problem for us. As you know, we have never allowed it to be an issue in our philanthropic society. The only other problem I foresee, Raina, is that your face will draw unwanted attention. That platinum hair, big blue eyes and gorgeous angelic face is just too enticing."

Raina wrinkled her nose at her older sister. "Listen to the pot calling the kettle black. Your mass of jet ringlets, black eyes and curvy figure," she paused and thought for a moment, "well it used to be curvy before this new pregnancy."

"And I love my little baby bump. I'm not going anywhere, outside the valley is not for me," laughed Catherine. "Back to the problem though of your looks. Let me think for a moment."

Raina and Sean stood silent, side by side, waiting for their leader's decision.

"Hmm, Sue Pimentel has that beauty shop in Spring Creek. We've been friends for a long time. She may have some really good ideas. Sean, may I use your cell phone, mine is encrypted too, but I don't know who will answer Sue's phone. She's got a houseful of kids, including teenage girls who are curious creatures."

Sean immediately handed over the small device.

"Ah, Sue, this is Catherine. I'm glad you answered your phone. Yes, everything is okay, Alexa is wonderful and the pregnancy is going well. Yeah. I'm getting to look like I ate a tennis ball. Yeah," Catherine listened for a couple of minutes.

"Actually, I need a quiet favor. Yes, a quiet one and the sooner the better. Raina needs to go awanderin' but she's too gorgeous by half. Can you tone her down a little, maybe dial back some of that beauty to make her fit in the outside world?" She listened for several minutes, then said, "As normal as possible please. Yeah. Sean. Sean McKinney. Just a moment I want the others to hear so I'll put it on speakerphone."

"Raina? Sue Pimentel. When do you need for this to be done?"

"As Catherine says, as soon as possible please," answered Raina.

"It's close to two o'clock now, can you be here by four? I can change Mrs. Jacobson's appointment to tomorrow with no problem and all the kids are at an after-school program."

Raina turned to Catherine to gain permission. At her nod she answered, "Mrs. Pimentel that would be wonderful. We can come at four. Thank you so much."

"You are welcome. Good, that will give me time to think of some options for you. Oh, and come in the back door of the shop. No one else will be here just as Catherine asked."

"Thanks, Sue. I owe you one," Catherine replied.

"Catherine, if I did one quiet favor a week for the rest of my years I would not be able to pay you back. Call if you have need of anything else," she added as she hung up.

Raina lifted an eyebrow in question.

"A happenstance. Accidentally Seeing of one of her children headed for a destructive situation. Enough said. Both of you be sure to pack some older clothes for physical work. You can buy whatever else is appropriate for where you're going. Again, I remind you to be sure to take enough cash as our cards could be traced. And Raina, I do love you, and I'll miss my little sister for however long you are gone."

"And I'll miss you more. I thought this valley with all its secrets would be my place for all time. Now Sean and I will go awanderin'. Love you and we'll stay in touch."

CHAPTER FIVE

"Raina, are you serious? That's pretty drastic," Sean said in an appalled voice. "And it'll take years to grow back. Can't you do something else? A wig or something?"

Mrs. Pimentel held up a handful of stick-straight platinum and light gold hair, letting the silky mass run through her fingers. "Sean's right, Raina. It will take years for all this hair to grow this long again. You have to be absolutely sure. Once its cut, we can't put it back."

"Mrs. Pimentel, I need to look as normal as possible. All that hair draws a lot of attention. As Catherine explained, it's important that we not draw anyone's notice to ourselves wherever we go. We can't do anything about Sean's looks so we need to change mine as much as possible."

Both women turned to gaze at the tall twentyish male with his dark auburn hair and lightly freckled face. His six foot three carried no excess weight on his well-built frame.

"Ah, no. Whatever you're thinking Raina, the answer is no. No. And no. I'm not dyeing my hair, anyway the freckles would still be there. I do admit that they've gotten lighter over the years."

"Okay," sighed Raina, giving up on changing Sean's looks. "Cut it, Mrs. Pimentel, please. It's just hair. It will grow back. I need to look completely different and quite frankly I need to feel differently too. It's growing up time and the hair goes first."

"Okay, Raina. In for a penny in for a pound as old Granny would say." She picked up her brush and then she carefully pulled the hair back to the nape of Raina's neck. "Let's at least have something good come of this. It's so long that I'm going to braid it so I can cut it straight across and save it for the 'Love for Locks' program. They will match the hair and donate it to a cancer patient who needs it. Now you're still sure that you want it cut in the style you picked from the hair styling book?"

"Yes. And dyed that mousey brown color, please."

Nothing could be heard except the snipping sound of the scissors. "I'll just bag this," Mrs. Pimentel said. "Sean, why don't you go sit in the little office until I'm finish. It's going to take a while. And all you're fidgeting is driving me crazy."

"Glad to. I feel like I've contributed to the delinquency of beauty and I'll be punished severely somehow. The farthest away is where I want to be until this is all over. And I may be sick."

Forty-five minutes later, Raina called for him to come back in. "How do I look?"

"Who the hell are you, and what did you do with Raina? That plain brown hair in that shaggy cut is like nothing I've ever seen. And your face is different."

"Then we've succeeded. The cut is called a pixie cut, but with Raina's oval face some modification gives her a 'nothing' like appearance. Her face is different because I taught her to use a yellow base make-up to make her face look shallow."

"She doesn't look like she did. She's not ugly exactly but she certainly isn't drop-dead gorgeous like she really is either."

"Would anyone give me a second look? And be honest. This is too important."

Sean studied her carefully. "No. No, they wouldn't. You look okay but nothing outstanding."

"Good," replied Mrs. Pimentel. "A couple of other things and we should be good. A pair of brown lightly-tinted glasses with wrap-around brown frames should distort those big blues. Now, where did those girls put the rest of that stuff? They keep some of their drama makeup in these upper cabinets to keep them away from the little ones who always want to smear themselves with makeup. Ah, here it is."

She brought down a little cardboard box, opened it and took out a thin strip of sticky plastic. "The older girls were

Frankenstein's wife last Halloween and used these. Sean, watch carefully because you will have to reapply these occasionally although the girls say they don't come off easily."

With one finger she smeared a reddish paste down Raina's cheek blending it until it was smooth. She then placed a razor-thin, one-inch-long strip in the center, pulling Raina's eyelid down and continuing with the strip until she pulled the edge of her mouth up. The perfect face now looked like it had been in an accident, but had good plastic surgery, leaving only minor scarring and puckering in a state of healing.

"Mrs. Pimentel you are a genius. I don't even know me. Thank you, thank you."

"You will not be recognized as Raina Ramsey, sister to Catherine and Brenna Ramsey that's for sure," agreed Sean. "Truth is I wouldn't recognize you either."

Both Raina and Sean hugged Mrs. Pimentel, thanking her profusely when they left.

Driving out of Spring Creek toward the freeway, Sean explained, "I'm going to have to get used to you looking like that. Catherine said for us to keep this older SUV as long as we are traveling. She will personally off-line it from the fleet. Oh, and she'll have a couple of the flying mechanics from Sanhicks Airport pick up the little helicopter immediately and return it to Sanhicks,"

Clasping her hands in her lap, Raina nodded at her best male friend. "I will never be able to repay you, Sean. Never. Being the younger sister of Catherine and Brenna Ramsey is not easy, and yet it's wonderful. They now live happy lives with wonderful husbands and children. I have to admit that sometimes when I'm melancholy, I'm almost envious. I would have happily lived in Shadow Valley for the rest of my life if Kamon and I had mated. In my own mind that's what I had planned."

"Do you want to talk about it? It's a 300 plus mile drive to Oklahoma."

"No. At least not now. It's over. Obviously, our relationship was a figment of my very fertile imagination. No more tears."

"Done. Pact," Sean said giving her a high-five. "We won't mention the past until you want to talk about it. But if you ever want to talk you know that I will listen. And if you ask, I'll tell you the truth as I think it is."

"Thanks, Sean."

She blew out a breath slowly ruffling her new bangs, her thoughts in turmoil. Was I too young? Too damn innocent or was there just no chemistry for him with me? That all elusive chemistry so necessary to a relationship and can't be manufactured. Just because I wanted him, to touch and hold didn't mean he felt the same way about me. I even loved the smooth skin and his unique man smell.

They went through a drive-through fast food restaurant in a larger town to order hamburgers and cokes. Later they stopped for gas before they got back on the road, neither of them wanting to spend extra time getting to Oklahoma. Sean drove and Raina looked out the car window, both silent with their own thoughts.

It was late when they checked into a motel in a small town. Sean asked for connecting rooms and registered them as brother and sister, Shane and Anna Donovan. Catherine had suggested they travel as siblings, where fewer questions would be asked. He explained to the elderly man that his sister was recovering from an auto accident. The elderly clerk barely glanced at Raina sitting in the car, nodded, and handed him two keys.

Sean and Raina grinned at each other when he returned to the car. "It worked," Sean beamed. "He didn't even really notice you. No gawking or looking impressed. Raina, for the first time in your life, I think you are anonymous."

They rose early the next morning and drove thru another fast food drive-in for breakfast. Both Raina and Sean were comfortable in each others company so the continued silence didn't bother either of them.

Raina's thoughts and emotions were all over the place. She refused to dwell on yesterday's disaster. She pushed it away to concentrate on the positive aspects of her future as she couldn't do a damn thing about the past. A large part of her was elated to have the freedom to travel where she and Sean chose. The adventures that could possibly be in front of them. New people to meet.

When tears started to threaten, she turned to Sean and asked, "Does the same rules apply that we've always had? You, me and Liam? That it's just between us and no sharing if we ask?"

"Absolutely. Catherine would murder us in our sleep if she found out half the things we've shared, including teaching you to fly before your twelfth birthday."

"I've changed my mind. I want to talk, and for someone to tell me the truth."

"Same rules apply. An honest opinion even though it might hurt. Our everyday life outside the valley has to remain secret for the good of all."

"Was it me? Did I do something that turned Kamon off?"

Sean was thoughtful for a couple of minutes before he answered. "Of course, I don't know but you've always been the little general. Grandmother Ramsey said you were born a leader. You know what to do and just do it, so that can't be it."

"Why not?" asked Raina raising an inquisitive now-brown eyebrow.

"Think about it for a minute, Raina. It wouldn't make sense to resent something that someone had little to no control over. That would be as insane as not liking someone because of their eye color, or the color of their skin, or some equally inane thing they were born with. Something they had no control over."

"You're right, that would be just stupid. Other people say I am pleasant to look at, so does he not like that, you think?"

"Get real, Raina. You're drop-dead beautiful with pale hair, dark brows and lashes. Your face is angelic, even if your mind isn't. Of course, you're not pretty now, but he doesn't see you now."

"Thanks, I think. Then …."

"What do you know about Kamon? About his past, I

41

mean?"

"He's lived off and on with Grandfather Youngblood ever since I can remember. He's lived with him almost full time since Grandmother Youngblood died. I guess I never really thought about it. He's just always been Kamon. The person I absolutely adored."

"Then you don't know his background," he went on. "According to my mom, he came to Shadow Valley with Grandfather Youngblood when he was about four or five years old. Few people except Grandmother and Grandfather Youngblood know of his parent's history. Maybe Catherine and Brenna. No one talks about it. And Raina, you and I both know how much our early lives affect us, forevermore. What we see in the valley is very little of his past I think. And he leaves for a few days or weeks at a time still doing work for MAC. And we both know that MAC is a clandestine group of odd individuals that correct what is considered wrong, often very dangerous things."

"Well, he was in some sort of special armed force unit for several years I know. He came back to spend more time at Shadow Valley when I was about thirteen and home for a school vacation. I thought he was the most beautiful warrior I'd ever imagined."

"My Dad said he served in a Special Operation Unit that was so secret that most military leaders didn't know about it. My Dad was already in the Diplomatic Service stationed in France at the American Embassy with the highest clearances, and he didn't know exactly what Kamon was doing. And Kamon is a cousin of my mother's. Dad told Liam and me that Kamon had eventually left the special service unit and did some work in the enforcing group for MAC. Liam and I were scared to death of him. Dad told us that we should be. That he was coldblooded, ruthless, and could be a mean SOB."

"I didn't know that. That isn't the Kamon I know," Raina admitted. "All I saw was his personality at Shadow Valley when I was there at the same time as he was. I knew that he grew up with Catherine and Brenna, but being ten years younger and away at school, I wasn't part of that group at all."

"From the time that Liam and I started spending more and more time at Sanhicks Airport I've heard bits and pieces of Kamon's exploits for want of a better word. I know that he was a very young recruit serving as an interpreter in Bosnia, Russia, and Iraq, and was also at the Navy base in Guantanamo. And then there's that ambush with Gavin O'Neill when O'Neill killed your cousin Diane, where he got those facial scars."

"I knew about the attack that caused the scars, but not any of the rest. And only vaguely."

"After that attack, he left Shadow Valley for about a year, you were away at school I guess. Anyway, it was whispered that he had spent that year in China learning some sort of secret fighting system so that he would never again be caught without a weapon."

"I don't understand the without a weapon part."

"I guess that besides a knife, O'Neill had a gun and Kamon was empty-handed. In China he was taught a different kind of martial arts unified movement that is potent and deadly. It's one of those martial art skills that goes back for thousands of years. MAC set it up for him."

"Another thing I didn't know," murmured Raina.

"Uh, it seems to me that you really don't know the man Kamon very well. He really can be merciless and coldblooded. That's what makes him such a good ceaan-cath for Catherine. And the highly intelligent warrior he is. He seems to be able to set aside emotions and react Spock-like. All cerebral and ruthlessly physical. And he's secretive, doesn't share well, nor does he communicate if he chooses not to. And truthfully, I don't know if he is a good mate for you or not."

"I didn't know all his past and probably never will, but I did love him. My young heart adored him actually. And I wanted him as a man, a forever joining. All the things you mentioned only make him a warrior I can respect. I can appreciate the Protector and Warrior part of him more than most I guess. Now I will learn that life and love move on. Thanks for listening, Sean," she sighed as she closed her eyes feigning tiredness.

CHAPTER SIX

Exiting his pickup, Kamon stepped out onto the road to gaze out at Shadow Valley. Another Indian summer day before the start of true fall. To him, there was nowhere on earth that was more beautiful than the green valley hugging the sides of Sky Mountain. A hundred shades of green trees mingled with dashes of dirt brown. The greens and golds of early foliage vied with the darker hues of vines as they climbed to meet a crystal blue sky. The wide open sky and the basin of the Shadow Valley tightened his chest to aching tenderness. The belonging of Mother Earth and Father Sky meeting within Nature's beauty.

This was home. The place where his soul was rooted like a strong oak tree and his breath came easier. Only here could he banish the memories of other people's minds he had Walked through. The depravities and betrayals. The fanatics and pure demons. Here they melted like will-of-the-wisps, the early morning mist in the deep ravines.

He had worked and lived for a short time in many other places but this place called to his spirit, independent and wild. Tangled emotions that made his eyes sting. By opening his heart, he could almost hear the ancient drums of long-ago ancestors beating in time with the soft pounding of moccasins as they moved though the forest.

All troubles seemed smaller here beneath Sky Mountain. Here was the belonging he sought. That he needed like his next breath. The hellish week he had melted away as easily as late spring snow. He took a deep breath thankful for this refuge. Here his job of protector took the primary role over his emotions. All the trials of the last week diminished here. Here he was needed.

Where his heart sang. Here he was Kamon Youngblood and belonged.

He parked under the giant oaks sheltering the massive Stone House, a huge manor house similar to their original Scottish counterparts. The original Stone House was built in the early 1800"s by some long ago ancestors. Local stones were hauled from the river to be used to build a three-level structure much like the manor houses left behind in the old country. Stone House was a huge residence spreading over more than an acre of land, backed up to sheer mountain cliffs, and guarded overhead by giant oaks. The interior offices, meeting places, apartments and everything else was constantly in a state of remodeling to meet the requirements of the present occupants.

He entered the house through the back door near the kitchens to seek out Mrs. Searle. The middle-aged woman with the ink-black dyed hair insisted she was the housekeeper. In truth, she was the quiet mother hen who knew where everyone was, and what they were into. For him she was the most important informational post at the Stone House.

Four minutes later he was running up the stairs to talk to Catherine.

Kamon stomped into Catherine's office not bothering to knock on the door frame. "Where the hell is Raina? I just talked to Mrs. Searle's who was going up to check her room. She say's that Raina packed a couple of suitcases and left. She says she doesn't know where she went. That Raina wouldn't say. Is that true? Where did she go? What the hell is going on?" he shouted.

"And a Good Morning to you too, Kamon. To answer your question since you asked it in such a civilized manner, yes, Raina packed two suitcases and did not tell Mrs. Searle where she was going. She left with my permission however," Catherine's voice held a touch of sarcasm laced with anger.

"Gone? Gone where? Why the hell?" He asked loudly as he plunked down on a nearby chair, deflated. "Who's she with? Did she go to the Island?"

"Do you want to yell or talk? If you are finished yelling, I'm

46

willing to talk to you. If you continue raising your voice to me, you can leave. And I do mean that," Catherine stated in a seldom-used stern voice.

Running agitated hands through his hair, Kamon apologized, "I'm sorry, Catherine. I know better than to upset you, especially now with your new pregnancy. Can you tell me about Raina? Please." He left the sentence open ended.

"Raina is safe. She asked to leave, and Sean petitioned to leave with her. No, she is not on the Island, or on any other of our lands. She says she's going awanderin', going where the breeze blows as Grandfather Youngblood used to say."

"What? And you let her? My God, Catherine! Are you crazy? Anything could happen to her. She's young and headstrong and ..." he took a breath to continue yelling.

"And this is the last time I will warn you about raising your voice to me Kamon. Or you can leave." She stopped to stare angrily at the agitated man before she continued in a quiet voice. "If you can't stop your immature reactions and gain some self-control, then leave now. Raina is more than twenty years old. A very smart, well educated twenty-year-old. She asked to leave and she has the right if she wishes, as you well know. She's not your prisoner. Nor is she mine. I am thankful that Sean was willing to go with her to act as bodyguard."

"Sean? He's her Protector? I'll call him," he said jumping to his feet. "Why did she leave? When did she leave? Did something happen here? She didn't say goodbye to anyone according to Mrs. Searle's."

"You will not call him and that is an order. He is not your subordinate. Sean will take good care of her. He's certified by the Warrior Society as you well know. In fact, the Warrior Society had meant for Sean or Liam to be Raina's protector instead of you. As far as to why, you don't have the need to know." She lifted her chin to stare directly into his face.

Kamon was shocked. The gentle soft-spoken woman he had grown up with was now a steely-eyed leader willing and able to confront him. And win. The fight went out of him. She was right. He did not have the need to know. Only a soul-searing want to know. Only a bone deep need to assure himself that she was safe and protected. Not willing to share his chaotic emotions even with Catherine, he purposely groused, "She draws trouble with her looks like honey draws flies."

"Her beauty is also none of your concern," Catherine said stiffly. "You are no longer responsible for her well being, physically or emotionally. What you are is second-in-command of this tribal clan, and my long time childhood friend. Please fulfill those roles. I repeat, Raina is no longer your responsibility."

"Damn Catherine, I am sorry. I know not to push you. Trent would have my head if he knew I had upset you. This was just the last straw in a hellish week." He gave a deep heartfelt sigh. "The lumber for the Baker's house came in but it was all the wrong size. Every damn piece of lumber was cut inches too short which puts the building schedule off by who knows how long. Susan and A.J. are pushing to get into their house before winter and Susan is driving me crazy with changes she wants in the house plans."

He blew out another long breath. "Then wild pigs got into the Henderson's garden that I had promised to check on while they were gone. The entire garden is ruined. I checked with the Middleton family to see if they had any excess vegetables, and thankfully they do. And then the baby calf I've been nursing along for several days died yesterday morning, and the lady I *was* seeing decided to up the ante on our relationship."

"I sincerely hope that wasn't in the order of importance to you, Kamon." Catherine's face remained serene but there was a hint of laughter in her eyes.

"Unfortunately, it was close. Probably the baby calf dying would have honestly come first."

"Now I'm sorry. Do you want to talk about any of it?"

"Not really. The calf is dead, and the lumber will get here as soon as possible I guess. The architectural drawings are finished and everything else is ready to go. Susan's changes won't be a huge setback, and the Middleton boys helped clean up after the wild pigs, although the feral pigs are getting to be a dangerous nuisance. As to the lady I've been seeing, well it's hard to admit the truth, but I'm not interested in taking my relationship with Mary Jo to another level. Not on a long-term basis at least, as you well know. Short term suited me just fine."

"I didn't know you were in a relationship as you call it."

"I've been seeing Mary Jo for three months or so," he admitted. "She's a widow who lost her husband in an auto accident a couple of years ago. A friend from Spring Creek introduced us. She swore that she just wanted a temporary non-binding liaison, and that suited me just fine. Now she's decided that she wants a permanent relationship that includes a ring on her left finger. I like her but that's it. She's a good companion and easy to be with. And I can't go there with her. No, erase that. I don't want to go there with her. Ever."

"Kamon you're such a guy," Catherine grinned, shaking her head. "I know you are serious, but most women want it all, and that means for the relationship to go somewhere, preferably forward into a commitment."

"Can't go there with her," he reiterated, "I'm not that interested. Short term is all that I have in me."

"Then it's a good thing she called it off sooner rather than later then. A permanent joining is serious business as you well know."

"I know, but she wasn't the right one. It worked for the time. Catherine, you're my best friend. You know more about me than anyone now living. At thirty-one, people keep pushing me to settle down and start a family like you and Brenna. I can't go there. I don't know how to be as you are. And in some ways, I do not want to know how."

"You and I both know that marriage is not for everyone. But…?"

Ignoring the leading question, Kamon went on, "What's most important to me right now is being sure that all the clans

49

I'm overseeing are safe. Which brings me back to the original question. Where the hell is Raina? How can I help protect her if I don't even know where she is? Sean's good, but Raina is a trouble maker of the first degree, drawing every man within a hundred-mile radius. Now where is she, damn it?"

"As Raina would say, none of your damn business." Turning her back on him, Catherine marched toward the door. Turning around to face him she declared, "Okay, Kamon, I've given you as much leeway as possible. You chose to keep Raina as a lovely to look at teen. That's your bad and mine. She's almost twenty-one and an adult. Now leave her the hell alone. She is yours no longer. Period. This is your last warning," she declared as she left her small office to enter her communication center, shutting the door firmly behind her.

Kamon stood looking after her, completely stunned. Never in all their years they had known each other had she threatened him. And he knew she meant every word she had said. But how could he not worry about Raina? He wanted to continue asking about her but knowing Catherine, she would probably have him thrown out. Maybe not just out of Stone House but also Shadow Valley. And any argument with her was not winnable. She also sounded exceedingly angry with him. And disgusted.

He walked slowly out, exasperated but unsure what to do next. Raina was a constant in his life, worrying about her was as natural as breathing. She was a complicated, opinionated minx that turned him inside out, and left him wanting. And wanting was exactly not the right thing between them. Her light-hearted teasing and flirting along with her naïve touching might make him breathless, but the gap between their ages and experiences were too much to ever overcome. Passion and desire were foreign words to her. And the intensity of his would scare the living hell out of her.

The innocent must be protected at all cost. A bitter lesson he had learned as a child, and later in a village in Afghanistan. He shook his head slightly to dislodge thoughts of the troubled past, a trick Grandfather Youngblood had taught him.

Then he deliberately let himself remember when he had first seen Raina Ramsey, not as a child but as a potent beautiful teen. One that had made his hands sweat and his heart pound. He had been on leave from a covert action in Pakistan where he had interrogated a group of men who had raped and killed several very young innocents. As an intelligence operator with a special forces group, he was brought in by MAC only after all normal negotiations failed. What men did to other people in the name of religion was barbaric, and delving into their minds for reasons behind their butchery made him feel vile and unclean. But he did what he had to do as a Mind Walker, delve into the filth and discover the guilty ones.

As a twenty-four-year-old he had seen too many horrific acts in his Mind Walking. He had needed the R and R to immerse himself in the serene green hills of Shadow Valley on Sky Mountain where innocence was safe and protected. Where he could regain some of his soul that had leaked out along with parts of his humanity. Shadow Valley was a refuge for those who needed the isolation to reclaim themselves and regain their losses. People like him.

That day he had walked from Grandfather Youngblood's house to a meeting with Grandmother Ramsey. Raina had been standing in front of the Stone House. It was as if she was bathed in sunlight, her uplifted face a mask of serenity as the warmth of the sun beat down on her. She looked like light itself, all glowing and radiant with life. Shimmering sunshine. Shadow Valley's sunshine.

His breath had caught and he had felt faint. She was incredibly beautiful with pale platinum and gold hair falling to her waist, sky blue eyes with dark brows and lashes. He had seen her as a child on his brief visits, and knew she was twelve or thirteen years old. Now she was a child-woman on the cusp of change.

She would need protecting. His life-time work.

That had been a lifeline for him. Protector he knew how to be. Anything else between them was so far off-limits as to be unimaginable.

Pushing his thoughts aside with difficulty, he concentrated on the present. Someone had to know something about Raina and Sean. It was only a matter of finding that person without clashing with Catherine. He went over in his mind his choices. Trent, Catherine's businessman husband, was currently in New York dealing with his business empire so he probably knew nothing. And wouldn't tell him if he did. Kelly Pierce, a close friend and cousin, had moved to one of the Islands in Scotland so he wouldn't know.

Mr. MacPherson was in Edinburg doing something for Catherine, but he might be back by now. First though, he would talk to Liam McKinney, the twin of Sean McKinney, and then he would try to find Mr. MacPherson.

With a goal in mind, he strode quickly from the house in search of Liam. He found him at Sanhicks Airport, the very private secret airfield built into the side of Sky Mountain.

"What the hell do you mean you haven't a clue where Sean and Raina are? Has the entire valley gone nuts? Sean is your twin brother. You have to know!" Kamon's frustration boiled over, his voice becoming increasingly angry.

"Well, I sure as hell don't and stop trying to intimidate me," shouted Liam. "I know nothing. Sean did not talk it over with me. He didn't even say goodbye. He told Catherine to tell me that he needed to go with Raina. That's it. Nothing else. No other messages. Not to me or anyone else as far as I can find out. His cell phone is not answering. He's turned off the tracking device that we just modified. Raina's is off too."

"Then they don't want to be found. Damn it!" Running his hands over his face, Kamon groaned, "Between the two of them I don't know which I'm the angriest with, Raina for leaving or Sean for helping her leave."

"Well, I'm damn hurt that my twin and best friend didn't see fit to let me know he was leaving either. He could have at least told me he was Raina's new bodyguard. Instead, nothing. Kamon, you know Raina is safe with Sean. He will protect her with his life as we have sworn to do."

"I know Sean will keep her safe, or the Warrior Society wouldn't have sealed your pact. I just want to know where the hell she is!"

"Well, they didn't take a plane or a copter. I already checked that too. In fact, I've checked everything I can think of to check."

"Too bad," Kamon commented sourly. "With all the new tracking devices you two have put on those planes they would have been easier to find if they had used one of the planes." Trying another line of reasoning he asked, "Does he have to come back anytime soon to finish whatever you two were working on?"

"Not really. We had just finished modifying that new engine for Boeing so we're not super busy right now. I could have used his help with the drones though, and the engine Lockheed wants us to look at. Sean's been restless for awhile. He works okay outside the valley, better in some ways than I do."

"So does Raina," murmured Kamon softly.

"Are you going to look for them then?" asked Liam curiously. "Catherine told me to literally butt out. And she meant it."

"She told me that I didn't have the need to know. And no, I'm not going to look, as much as I want to. I'm not willing to upset Catherine anymore that I already did."

"Smart," was Liam's only comment.

Kamon didn't bother to tell him that he would talk to Mr. MacPherson who knew most of the happenings of the valley. He wasn't going to look for Raina and Sean but he could check to see if anyone else knew where they were.

Kamon also didn't add that he was beginning to agree that Raina had to spread her own wings to fly. Even if he wasn't included in her flight plan. Damn it to hell.

CHAPTER SEVEN

"**D**idn't take her long did it?" grinned Brenna gazing across the mountain of rubble that had once been a house. Everything from sticks to parts of a washing machine to indistinguishable items looked like it had been stirred by the giant hand of the tornado. And all of it dirty, grimy, or mangled beyond restoring.

Raina stood talking to an older man wearing a FEMA coverall, both of them wearing yellow hard hats to distinguish them as government workers. Raina gestured at several of the volunteers clearing debris, and then listened as the older man nodded his head in agreement. She touched his arm lightly as she walked away.

"No, it didn't take long." Cocking his head to the side, he asked softly, "Have you noticed something different about Raina? She's … I don't know. Different. Maybe more independent now. Changing somehow, becoming more. I think not being taken care of constantly is good for her."

"Yeah, Deke and I were talking about it. Raina has always been put in a box. A very beautiful box, and it gave her needed protection, but it also didn't allow her to expand. To grow into her self. She's going to be something unique," Brenna grinned. "I think its even more than that. I've always thought that people were drawn to her because of her striking looks. Now, I don't think so."

Sean raised an eyebrow, waiting for Brenna to continue.

"There's something in medicine called pheromones which makes people of the same species react differently toward whoever. It's that 'IT' factor. The un-namable reason that the eye is drawn to certain people. And it's so subtle that it happens without anyone's awareness. I think Raina may have been given an extra helping of that. Even with the ugly haircut, scar and dirty clothes, people are still drawn to her."

Both continued to watch as Raina walked toward them.

"Hello, sister of mine," Raina smiled, joining Brenna and Sean. She was only shades cleaner than Sean, which didn't say much. Gesturing toward the piles of wreckage that had once been a home, Raina said ruefully, "I know it looks like we've done very little, but actually it's coming along very well."

"The Hawkins family has been here and scoured the area for any mementos or anything else of value to them," she continued. "They found an old metal box of pictures, that was about the only things left that were salvageable. The volunteers are sorting the rest into piles. Some of the wood can be recycled, and anything else that someone else could use, or the Hawkins want back, will be sorted. Mostly now it's waiting for Sean and Deke's bulldozers to load the remaining trash into dump trucks for this section." She gazed in satisfaction at the site. Mountains of debris were piled up and down the street.

"How long have you been here, Raina? Five days? Six? And you've somehow organized the volunteer group of individuals into a cohesive working group. You are amazing, sweetie." Brenna put her arm around her younger sister for a quick hug.

"I'm going to get you really dirty," grinned Raina. "Your clothes are clean and those dark blue hospital scrubs and gleaming white leather shoes are going to stay clean out here for about three minutes. And you, Sean, are even dirtier than I am. You look like you have been dumpster diving, even your red hair is covered in the gray-brown dust of this area."

"Looks like you've got it organized though,'" commented Sean.

Raina laughed lightly. "The easy part was organizing the volunteers to work together instead of each of them picking up something and being clueless where to put it. They all want to help and have donated their time to do so. Oh, and I also have to remember to answer to Anna and call Sean by Shane when I talk to him. I'm always afraid that I will slip-up and say, 'Who'?"

"It was a good idea. I can remember the name Shane as its close to Sean. Catherine could have said Mortimer or Thaddeus," grinned Sean.

"Funny! Catherine suggested we use those names as ours are too distinctive. And our new names belong to one of our long-ago ancestors which is kind of like role playing." Raina waved a hand toward the older man walking toward a FEMA truck.

"The other hard part of coordinating the volunteers was convincing that FEMA government man, Mr. Horton, that all this organization was his idea. Oh, and that he needed to take the credit. Accordingly, I work under him and all the organizational work is his," she grinned in remembrance. "It amazes me that someone would care who gets credit for cleaning up this disaster that has hurt so many people. So many of them have nowhere else to go. They're literally homeless."

"I know," Brenna replied, "we see them at the hospital. They look shell-shocked, and in truth most of them are."

"Yeah, I've talked to some of the families. The Edward's family have three children under five with few family resources. They are staying with some people across town who offered to take them in, which is incredibly kind, but a temporary fix. Some of the people hit by the tornado have insurance, and most others will be eligible to disaster relief of some sort I hope."

"We do what we can, Raina," Brenna assured her. "It will never be enough and there is always another disaster looming that has more needs. Mother Nature wreaks havoc on us poor mortals."

"Well, Mr. Horton says that all the attention this tornado disaster has received will be advantageous when he requires more money. If he needs the awareness from good old Washington, D.C. to think he's great so they can give him more resources for rebuilding, I'm all for it. I've finally convinced him to go for it. I certainly don't want to be involved in all that."

"And we don't need the attention." Sean reminded her, grimacing as he rolled his sore shoulder muscle.

"You okay?"

"Yeah, just too much lifting I guess. Out of shape."

"Are you two about finished for today? It's been really busy. Tomorrow is my last day at the hospital, I'm just going to hang out and play with Brandon until Deke is finished. Most of the severely injured have been treated or moved to a Medical Center in Oklahoma City. Medical students are arriving tomorrow for a couple of weeks to do follow-up under the supervision of their instructors. There will be a few scares and minor injuries still coming in, but the local physicians can handle the more serious injuries. Now I'm hungry, and Deke has Brandon who is always hungry," complained Brenna with a warm smile.

Raina had told her sister about Kamon and how hurt she felt. Brenna listened, gave her warm hugs, and no advice whatsoever. Exactly as Raina had requested. She had given Brenna permission to tell Deke so he understood.

"Speaking of your other-half-Plus, here comes your troops," kidded Sean. "At least Deke is dirtier than me."

"That's because I ate your dust most of the day. The wind was definitely on your side," grinned Deke, flashing a white smile in a dirty face. He carried the almost two-year-old Brandon on his hip. Deke's skin and clothes were a dirty brown as were his small son's overalls. Most of the little boy's skin was clean however, as he spent his days in the hospital's day care program. Deke put his arm around his wife, but kept Brandon in his arms.

"Mama, mama. Me ride tractor with Daddy!" shouted the exuberant little boy. "Tractor, mama, tractor."

"So much for not telling, Sport," laughed Deke. "It was a Cat and totally safe," explained Deke to his wife as she narrowed her green eyes at him. "He did get a tad dirty though. I washed him off as much as I could," he admitted, trying in vain to dust Brandon's shirt off as he set him on his feet.

Raina's heart warmed at the sight of the exuberant two-year-old, an almost a miniature of his father. Brandon's personality was also the easy-going style of Deke's own, nothing bothered Brandon except hunger which he did not tolerate.

"Hey, Raina. It's looking good. Almost ready for some removal?"

"Tomorrow for sure. I'm starving. Please tell me somebody cooked. Preferably you, Deke," Raina begged.

Sean and Raina had joined Deke, Brenna, and Brandon living in the recreational vehicle. It made sleeping arrangements tight, but motel accommodations were scare to none in the small town with so many residents and outsiders needing space to help with the disaster relief. The local motels had made a policy that residents hard hit from the tornado got first dibs on the available rooms.

Deke had bought the used RV in an adjoining town near the disaster area. It made a safe inside play area for Brandon and modest sleeping quarters for Brenna and himself. The space was a little crammed now with two more.

"You got lucky. I threw a roast and vegetables in the crockpot this morning. Somebody else needs to learn to cook," he grinned looking directly at his wife, then at Raina.

Brenna stuck her nose up in the air and said in a pretend haughty tone, "Not me. I'm pregnant."

"Not me, I don't know how," Raina said mimicking Brenna's haughty tone and tipped nose.

"The pregnant one makes me happy, but the other one needs to learn," chuckled Deke. "And Brenna, I'll be your cook forever if you give me a little girl. I want one who looks just like you and just as sassy."

"Ah, Deke, you do know that it's the man who determines the sex of the child? Right? That was part of your law enforcement training," teased Raina. "And I don't think sassy is what Brenna is. More like determined. Oh, and independent."

"Sassy is Brenna," he laughed happily. "Hey, I could have added willful, stubborn and ...."

"And you could have lots of rights revoked," teased Brenna lifting a dark brow.

They all laughed, Brandon along with them even though Raina knew that he was clueless to what was funny.

"Are you gong back to Spring Creek soon, or are you contracted with International Aid to volunteer somewhere else," asked Sean. "Raina and I are flexible right now, but Spring Creek is not on our itinerary, nor is Shadow Valley. Not for awhile anyway."

"Nope," agreed Raina, "not going there."

"Actually, neither are we. I need to go to the ranch in Texas when we're finished here," said Deke satisfaction lacing his voice. "Brenna needs to sleep about sixteen hours a day with this new pregnancy, and I need to check on the horses out there to see what I can trailer to the new Spring Creek ranch. There're a couple of good riding horses that we could use with beginners at Spring Creek."

"Horses, horses, Daddy. We ride, okay? Okay?" Brandon had jumped to his feet and was now tugging on his father's pant's leg at the magic word of horse.

"Soon, Scout, soon," Deke promised, giving the sturdy little boy a quick hug.

Raina smiled at the small family. Deke's sheer joy in his young son was a pleasure to watch. He never seemed to be too busy to take care of the little boy when Brenna was pressed for time. Nothing seemed to be beneath him with Brandon's daily care from potty training to story reading.

Deke had been in law enforcement and had tragedies shadowing his past. He was street-smart, tough, and physical. The training of the Warrior Society had only enhanced what he was; a six-foot four man with dark hair, hazel eyes and a lean muscular frame who had vowed to protect his wife against all comers. The love and happiness between the couple was palpable.

Brenna stood beside him leaning against his strength, her tiny baby-bump barely discernible under her hospital scrubs. Brenna was lovely, with auburn hair and grass-green eyes. Dr. Brenna Ramsey was the gifted healer of Clan Ramsey, using her unique abilities in secret to help as many sick people as possible.

"What?" asked Brenna. "You left us there for a moment."

"Truthfully, first I was admiring your family. And thankful that with both you and Catherine pregnant, there's going to be more babies to love. Secondly, I was laughing at me about my puffed-up self. Do you realize that not one person has questioned my appearance?" Raina smiled happily. "Not a single one. I've been around the same people for several days and they all assume that what they see is what is. I'm a normal person whose face has been altered by scars after an auto accident."

"Are you really okay with that?" asked Sean. "Knowing that underneath the dyed hair and plastic strip that you are pretty enough to garner major attention? It must be really different for you."

"At first it was disconcerting. I tried to hide, and then I realized that no one was looking at me. Of course it is different than what I've been used to, but it's also freeing, if that makes sense. I can stand on the sidelines and be an observer, instead of the center of attention. Watch what others are doing without being forced to interact with them. My looks are a part of me, but they no longer define me. Nor do they limit me. It's hard to explain so you can understand."

Deke and Brenna exchanged silent glances.

"I can sort of understand that," commented Brenna. "I am a healer, but I'm also the wife of Deke, and the mother of Brandon besides all the other responsibilities that are mine by birth. Sometimes in the past, the features that Grandmother passed to me have been a distraction from what I need to do, especially the copper hair."

"Your hair is glorious," replied her husband, his eyes warm as he looked down at her.

"Daddy, daddy, gotta' go potty," interrupted Brandon. "Now, Daddy. Now."

"Honestly he waits until it's an emergency before he tells anyone," chuckled Deke sweeping his son into his arms and hurrying toward the tiny RV bathroom.

"I think my two sisters are the luckiest ladies in the universe," beamed Raina. "Pregnant and with great husbands. And one of their men cooks, thank heavens. Life is good."

And it was. She had forced thoughts of Kamon to the recesses of her mind, not allowing him to gain traction in her new life. Reality and Shadow Valley were far away where she needed them to be for now. Later they could be taken out, mulled over, and examined, but not now. Now she needed to move forward. And take that one day at a time.

Two days later most of the cleanup had been organized into large piles of trash or reusable materials. Team leaders were chosen who were capable of implementing the overall plan that Raina had developed. Mr. Horton, the FEMA man, with Raina's not-so-gentle guidance, had chosen another volunteer supervisor to take Raina's place and to see that everything remained on track. The area would take months, and in some cases years, to rebuild as it had been before the tornado. If it ever was.

"Okay, Sean. My job here is winding down. I'd like to leave soon if that's okay, partner. I did tell Mr. Horton that if he ever had a drastic need for the two of us to contact Brenna at the International Medical Aid group. I hope you agree."

"I do agree but I've ate all the dirt I want for now," he added smiling. "How about us leaving in the morning? Deke and Brenna will only be here for another couple of days anyway."

"That works for me. I'd like to see more of the United States and feel less like a dirt person," Raina grinned, ineffectively brushing off her soiled shirt.

They left early the next morning, promising Brenna that they would go by Deke's ranch in Texas if at all possible at some point in their travels.

Now that Brenna was pregnant with her second child, she said she was going to volunteer less with the International Aid Society for disaster relief in other countries. Deke had just smiled spreading his large hands to indicate whatever she wanted. Brenna's work was lifesaving, and he was her very willing partner in whatever she did.

Brenna had told Raina about promises made and promises kept.

CHAPTER EIGHT

"**A**ny ideas where we should go to now? North? South?" Raina tried to smooth the wrinkles from her worn jeans with little success. Dust and dirt from the disaster site clung to all surfaces, especially to human skin. Getting clothes clean with water in short supply wasn't easy or effective.

"Yep, I've given it some thought. What would you think about taking a car trip and seeing the Southwestern part of the United States? I've flown over it and worked in some of the larger cities but I've never experienced it up close and personal. Wha'ca think?"

"Hmmm. That's a great idea. Wherever we wander is some-place new to me. Brenna touched up my hair before we left, so she says I'm good for a couple of weeks at least. And I have more dye when I need to touch it up, although I may need a little help."

Sean wrinkled his nose, "Hope it's not too soon. It's messy."

"Says the dirt man," laughed Raina. "Where you thinking from here? I have book knowledge of the geography of the United States and absolutely no experience."

"Well, I have very little ground experience, so this should be an adventure for both of us which is exactly what we wanted. We'll simply stop and see whatever catches our fancy. And keep our promise to Catherine to help when we can."

Raina thought back to how she had been able to handle the last weeks. One of the twelve steps in AA was to take one day at a time. She knew that she could get through one day no matter how much her heart hurt and her eyes stung. One day. Just one day.

The further away from Shadow Valley she traveled, the more unreal her former life became. Hours went by when there were no thoughts of Kamon, or even of Catherine. Maybe Catherine was right, Raina thought. I was infatuated with Kamon and too inexperienced to recognize what it really was. And I'm inexperienced in everything else in life too.

"You know Sean. Much as I hate to admit it, Deke was right that I do need to learn to cook and do the practical stuff. I know next to nothing about handling money, or cooking, or anything that most people grew up taking for granted."

"True. It's also true for me in some aspects. Mom is a diplomat's wife and takes care of Dad. We've always had a cook and housekeeper. And plenty of money."

Raina nodded in agreement. "I've lived most of my life in Shadow Valley where Mrs. Searle has taken care of us. When I was younger, a lot of people told me what to do, and I just did it. Whether it was to go to school, learn whatever was best for me to learn, and on and on. If I wanted something, I asked for it, and it was normally given to me. Now, if I want anything different, I've had the Shadow Valley stores, or I've simply gone down to Fortuna to pick it up."

"What are you thinking in that busy little brain of yours?"

"Sean, is it possible for us, especially me, to learn all the stuff most people were taught from babyhood? I feel so ignorant. And I hate the feeling."

"Truthfully, I don't know, but it would certainly be interesting to give it a shot. I'd love to work for money to see if we could earn our way but that's not possible."

"Why not? I'm a hard worker and it would certainly change the equation. We wouldn't have to get a really good job, just something to earn our own way, so why not?"

"Because it would put us on the radar with all the papers we would have to fill out. The government takes out taxes, keeps track of social security deductions, and a host of other things," he frowned in thought. "What we could do though, is to try to live as cheaply as possible as if we were earning our way."

Raina thought it over for a moment. "That would work, I think. It would certainly be a needed lesson for me."

"We have money if push comes to shove, as Grandfather said. But let's try it. If nothing else, we will learn things we don't even have the experience to know we don't know."

"Done," agreed Raina, high-fiving Sean.

The next three weeks was a time out of time for both Sean and Raina.

They crossed through Oklahoma into Texas, and traveled down the state stopping in San Antonio. The city of San Antonio was beautiful and lush with flowering plants and trees. Most of the buildings were of Spanish style architecture and pristine in their whiteness.

The first day they strolled along the meandering pathway of the waterway of the famous River Walk. They talked to a street musician who told them about the homeless shelter where he stayed. They spent a week serving breakfast, lunch, and dinner there plus cleaning up the kitchen in return for meals, and a shared dorm-type room. And they had an opportunity to talk with some of the residents.

Raina fluctuated between awe at the resilience of some of the residents of the shelter, and hopelessness in talking to others. All had a story. A large number of them needed health care and mental health care. Others were heavily addicted to alcohol or drugs. Some of them had only been one pay check from the streets most of their lives, and through no fault of their own, there was no paycheck now. They worried about the basics; safety, food, and shelter.

Some had families somewhere, but had lost touch, or as one old woman said, "I've messed up so badly that they don't want me around." A large number of them needed a hand up, and homeless might be temporary. There were some resources available, but never enough.

Sean fell in love with the tiny old lady named Gladys who ran the soup kitchen with an iron hand. She treated everyone as if they were highly paid employees, and Sean thought she was even bossier than Raina. She was also warm, funny, and gave out great hugs indiscriminately to volunteers, employees, and homeless people alike.

In between working at the shelter, they tried to see as much of San Antonio as cheaply as possible. They toured the Alamo fortress where a small group of Texans in the early days of 1836 had held out against 1500 of General Santa Ana's Mexican troops for 13 days before they were all killed.

Raina knew the history of the place, but the old adobe fort seemed steeped in sadness with the heroic resistance. She could almost feel the bloody battle raging as the Texan's fought for independence and General Santa Ana gave the orders of "no quarter". Knowing how many men died on both sides of the battlefield left Raina with a sense of melancholy.

"You know I could live here," Raina commented one afternoon as she sat sipping iced lemonade with her full plate of enchiladas and tacos before her. The view from their outside riverfront table was of the luxuriant river walk meandering toward the little lake where sailboats floated on the gentle wind of the waterway. The city of San Antonio reminded Raina of a Spanish flamenco dancer; colorful, flamboyant, mature, and exuberantly fun.

"Don't think you could afford to, you just spent one day's equivalent of our salary on that food. Besides, you would miss your family," Sean stated firmly. "The food though is incredible."

"You know Sean, you have no romance in your soul," Raina teased. "Look at that view."

"And you do? Yeah, right," laughed Sean. "San Antonio is beautiful, but not what would make either of us happy in the long run. I think our background has been too different. Shadow Valley and its isolation and privacy are still a balm for us. Something we both need. Maybe not all the time, but certainly sometimes."

"You know what I miss?"

"Raina, I wouldn't have a clue. I don't even know what you're talking about three-fourths of the time."

"I was thinking of the valley and I miss the Stone House.

I miss Maggie and Douglas and the mischief they somehow attract like mini-magnets. I love being a part of a small community, of knowing everyone. Even the grumpy people like Fergus," she admitted. "He may be a grump but he's my grump, if that makes sense. Oh, and I love my suite of rooms in that huge old rambling fortress. For me, it is like being enveloped in a giant's arms, safe, secure and never changing."

"Well, it doesn't change much that's for sure. The old ones built it of stone to make it last for hundreds of years like their castles and houses in the Highlands. Everyone lived inside the dozens of rooms, especially during crises or disasters. Remember when most of the children got the croup several years ago, and the downstairs was turned into a family hospital?" Sean sighed. "Yeah, we are very lucky to be part of the community even with its many warts and isolation."

"The worst for me is that most people see me as a twelve-year-old, somehow stunted from aging in the last eight years," Raina groused.

"For me, it's the lack of privacy. Honestly, three people know what I'm thinking before my thoughts are fully developed."

Raina and Sean's relationship had developed into a close sibling-like status, sharing thoughts and feelings at random. Sometimes they bickered, and sometimes they were so in tune with each other as to have no need for words to express their feelings. As cousins growing up together, they understood their pasts and respected the part the other played in that. Both were careful to not tread on unasked for ground however.

After two weeks they decided that it was time to move on toward New Mexico. They made a promise to Gladys to visit on their return if it was at all possible. They made short stops in various tiny towns in Texas but none of them seemed to need any help they could give. Raina found the little self-insulated communities fascinating as most of the inhabitants were related in some way, either directly or by marriage, much like Spring Creek except less populated.

Their roaming took them up to New Mexico and the large crossroad city of Albuquerque. The city was a unique mix of age-old Spanish and Native American architecture and new-world modern buildings.

Raina had thought that Albuquerque was made up of two distinct cultures, the Caucasian and the Native American cultures. She quickly learned that there was a third racial make-up which played prominently in the history of the area, the Spanish. Surprisingly there were some who had only Spanish blood, and many Native American with no Caucasian or Spanish roots at all. Instead of separate entities, the three cultures were intermingled in such a manner that sometimes only their history decided who did what with whom first. Many people were a combination of the three cultures, or a mix of one or the other. The Mexican culture of the mix was very much a part of the city.

The compact area of the old village of Albuquerque was a maze of gardens and courtyards. The historic adobe buildings held a plethora of quaint shops and first rate restaurants situated around the town square. The Old Town square was anchored by the 1793 San Felipe de Neri Church with its wooden pews and beveled stained glass windows. Dancers from the outlying Pueblo villages as well as local Spanish-inspired dancers gave free exhibitions for the tourists in the middle of the outside grassy square.

On a side street of the old town square was a pre-school ran by Catholic nuns where they both volunteered every morning. In the afternoon, Raina helped in the kitchen and Sean mowed lawns with a Hispanic man he had met through the pre-school. It was easy to find a cheap motel with a tiny kitchen in a relatively safe area in which to stay.

Raina had also decided she did need to learn to cook as Deke had suggested. She went into a large grocery store to look at cookbooks while Sean bought sandwiches from the Deli.

"Good grief. This cookbook costs $29.95," she exclaimed out loud. An older woman standing beside her laughed with her.

"Doesn't make sense, does it?"

"It doesn't, but I do need to learn how to cook something."

"Your mama didn't teach you?" the older woman asked with a lifted eyebrow.

"My mother died when I was young," commented Raina as she thumbed through the book.

"Well, you don't need any of those," the old lady said firmly looking at Raina's well worn clothes. "What you need to do is go down to the thrift store, and look through what they have. They don't cost much, maybe a dollar or two. And you need to get one with a lot of pictures. Or see if you can find one that teaches little kids to cook if you really don't know anything about it."

"Thank you, thank you," Raina beamed. "Where is the thrift store?" She didn't have enough courage to ask what a thrift store sold.

"Best one is down on Second Street. Go out to the street and turn left. Turn right on Second, it's on the right-hand side of the street down about a mile or so."

The thrift store was a treasure trove for Raina and Sean. Work clothes, lightweight jackets, books, anything and everything. Raina bought several beginner or "dummy" cookbooks, and Sean purchased several mystery books for reading during their downtime.

They wandered the streets of Albuquerque Old Town, feasting on the Mexican and Native American foods of the region, always keeping an eye on the costs. Both Raina's and Sean's favorite food were the sopapillas, the deep-fried dough of 'little pillows' often stuffed with honey to take away the heat of the spicy food. Knowing that she might never have a chance again, Raina bought beautiful silver and turquoise hand-crafted earrings for Brenna and Catherine from one of the Native American's selling their wares on the sidewalks of the plaza.

Another favorite place in Albuquerque was the Pueblo Cultural Center where the 19 Pueblo tribes had built a beautiful adobe center to showcase the accomplishments of the Pueblo people. Sean was fascinated by the adobe architecture while Raina could have spent days in the historical exhibits and the large retail shop attached. They shared an Indian taco which according to the menu was fry bread with chili beans, lettuce, tomatoes, salsa, and cheese. Altogether delicious. Sean and Raina were especially drawn to the museum's motto "Our Land, Our Culture, Our Story."

Lately, neither Sean nor Raina talked about Shadow Valley, or what had precipitated their trip. Kamon and the tribal clan were a world away. They did keep their promise to call Catherine every week, giving her highlights of where they were and what they had seen, knowing that the information was for her alone. They told her the stories of some of the people they had met and how different their lives were. They did not tell her that they were trying to live as cheaply as possible to get a different perspective of other people's lives.

No one looked askance at either of them. They tried to be exactly what they seemed, a large auburn-haired brother taking care of a non-descript little sister, working and sightseeing the American southwest. Raina hated to leave Albuquerque and the Land of Enchantment, and vowed to herself to come back someday if at all possible.

They talked over their next itinerary deciding on a short trip to the Grand Canyon and then to the Skywalk on the Hualapai Reservation. They were arguing about whether to try to stay in Flagstaff or go on to the Grand Canyon when Sean's phone rang.

"Hello. Okay, I'll put it on speakerphone level 7. It's Brenna," he explained.

"Sorry to interrupt your vacation but Mr. Horton, that FEMA government man, is trying to get in touch with you two," announced Brenna with regret in her voice. "He said that you both offered to help again if he needed it. And he says he desperately does."

They could hear Brenna blow out a long sigh. "Long story short. It seems that there was an earthquake in a little town between the coastline and the San Joaquin Valley in California. He said there's one death, many injured, and the center of the town is rubble. Deke absolutely forbids me going. The truth is they have a lot of medical help and don't need me. Stanford Medical Center is sending some of their residents and students down to help."

"What they need most right now is someone to organize the disaster area and that's you, Anna. He also mentioned how impressed he was that your brother was familiar with heavy equipment and could modify it to fit different situations, and that's you, Shane. I did not give him a definitive answer to whether you could come or not. I did tell him I would try to reach you and would call him back."

Sean looked at Raina hopefully. "What do you say, Raina? For me, I like to work on that equipment, and they do need us. Even if we don't want to stay for a long time, maybe we could help initially. I think that we should use more of our money from home now."

"I certainly agree with that. It's more important that we get there as soon as possible. We can break up our wandering for awhile, and then resume when we're not needed any more." She cocked her head to one side to concentrate on a map in her head. "We're about ten or twelve driving hours from there. We can take turns driving and be there early in the morning. Is that okay, Sean?"

"Sounds good. I'll take the first two-hour shift."

"Do you want me to call him back or do you want to call him?" Brenna asked interrupting their dialogue.

"Would you mind calling him? He has a tendency to be long-winded, and we need to make some plans."

"You two be careful, you hear?" Brenna demanded.

"Yes mama," they mocked in unison, grinning like loons. Another new experience.

CHAPTER NINE

Kamon waited in the front of the Stone House entryway. He was always awed by the entrance hall which opened to a three-story roofline. A massive iron chain holding a wrought-iron circular chandelier hung from the tall ceiling. The walls of stone were draped with antique silken banners depicting heraldic shields. Slate floors were covered with costly Persian carpets in faded jewel tones. Hand-carved ornate side tables held artifacts ranging from a priceless Ming vase to an ancient shield of silvered armor. Identical curving mahogany staircases led upward toward unseen rooms on each side of the entry. Massive mahogany doors, polished to a gleaming shine, bordered each side of the entry and were closed.

Catherine had called a special meeting of the Sgnoch Council, but had given no specifics of the emergency meeting.

He watched as Catherine walked slowly down the long hallway to the front of the Stone House. The beginning of the second trimester of this pregnancy seemed to make her balance off-center.

"You do know I'm fine, right Kamon? You really didn't have to escort me down the steps," Catherine smiled. "Although I do appreciate the thought."

"Of course I do, but just this once. I want to be sure those old stairs don't trip you up." He opened the heavy mahogany doors just off the entryway so they could descend the wide slate stairway to an older underground section of the house. The stairway walls were made of river rock washed smooth by the timeless tumbling of river flow.

He held her arm as she carefully put one foot in front of the other, holding onto the iron side railing with her other hand. It was much cooler here below ground. The landing at the bottom of the stairs faced a door that was ten feet high with thick wooden planks held together by handmade wrought iron cross bars. Giant hinges were attached to the door frame dark with age. The walls of the room were of river rock replicating the stair walls and outside hallways, blending smoothly with the grey slate floors. Huge timbers carved with unreadable symbols on the massive beams held the rough wooden roof. Clan business had been run from the ancient underground room for almost two hundred years.

Kamon pulled out Catherine's chair at the head of the long wooden table and carefully seated the clan leader. Seven of the nine members of the Sgnoch Council were seated at the long wood-planked table, only Brenna and Raina were missing. The back of each large wooden chair was heavily carved with cryptic symbols, no two alike. The only color in the room was the muted petit-point stitching on the chair cushions made by some long-ago person.

Kamon sat at Catherine's right. His mind reviewed his own status here in this special room. Here he was to serve and keep the members and all their associates safe. The destiny he had chosen for himself.

Kamon was responsible for the protection and security of the clan, its associates, and of clan businesses. Long ago the ancestors had set up a system that when physical strength was needed, a second in command was chosen by the leader; essentially a War Chief, a ceann-cath. Some Southwestern Native American tribes had some of the same strategies and traditions, especially when going to war. Many female leaders had successfully led tribes, in war and in peace even in the twenty-first century.

Next to Kamon, Raina's chair sat empty as did Brenna's along the line. Robert Neal occupied Kelly Pierce's seat temporarily, but was sure to be elected at the next quarterly meeting if he so wished. Kelly had asked to be relieved of Council duty to take a permanent position in Scotland. Aunt Ulla sat at the opposite end of the table from Catherine with Duncan Frasier on her right and next to him sat his cousin, John McDougal. Mary O'Reilly was between John McDougal and Mr. MacPherson. Nine members made up the Sgnoch Council, the decision making group running the ancient tribal clan empire. Many at the table held proxies for a multitude of associate clans. All members of the Council knew any personal problems did not follow them into this room. Clan business was too important for pettiness of the individual spirit.

"We have a difficult decision to make and I would like suggestions," Catherine stated without preamble. "But first, yes, Raina and Sean are fine after awanderin' for several months, and no they have no immediate plans to return, and no, you may not ask questions. Now to something extremely serious."

Kamon started to comment, then decided it really was not his business. One of the hardest things he had ever done was to let go of the responsibility of everyday caring for Raina Ramsey. He thought of her often throughout his day, but forced himself not to question Catherine. Catherine was right, he did not have the need to know. Only the want.

"I received a message this morning from MAC." She looked at each member of the Council. "It has been a long time since they've needed our help, usually it is their group handling difficult situations for us. They stated that it is vital that they have information from a prisoner in a California prison and asked for our assistance."

She waited for a moment before continuing, "They've tried the easier methods already. They've tried infiltrating the cell block he is in with "other prisoners" quote, unquote. They've tried bribery, both to his friends and his family, as well as to the prison guards. Everyone is too afraid to cooperate. MAC has even tried kidnapping the prisoner outright, but he is protected even inside the prison."

"The obvious question is why is this man so important?" asked Mr. MacPherson, clasping his elegant hands in front of his face.

"I was just coming to that. According to MAC, this man, Matteus, still runs a gang organization, even from his prison cell. This time it seems to involve the kidnapping of girl children from Mexico or Central America. Whether the children are to be used for prostitution, as drug mules, or as hostages for the M13 drug cartel or another group, no one knows. And no one can find out."

"This has gone to the highest level of our world, and MAC is stumped. They've even thought of blowing up the cell block with him in it which is their best idea right now. Unfortunately, they don't know if that would stop whatever is in the process of happening."

"What about the country where the girls live? Can the girls be protected by them?" Mary O'Reilly asked. Mary was a Harvard educated attorney whose specialty was negotiating with South American banks with tribal clan business ties.

"It doesn't appear that they are interested, or perhaps it would be more prudent to say that they don't have the ability to handle this kind of operation."

"Why MAC? Why is an essentially a mercenary group involved?" This from Mr. MacPherson, the business expert of the group, and the coolest head.

"They said that they owed a favor and this was pay-back. And they hate abuse, especially of children. It's not our job to speculate about their involvement. We have to help them if we can. Period. Our connection is too symbiotic to question. Any other ideas?"

"There's a prison hospital, Brenna might ...."

"Not only no, but as Trent would say, hell no! I'll call her after the meeting is over, but she sleeps all day with her new pregnancy, and has a two-year-old. And a husband that would blow up the entire prison himself if she even thought about becoming involved."

74

"Okay, okay, you're right," John McDougal grinned, holding his hand up in defense.

"Is there any way we could monitor his communication system? He has to have a means of connecting with his people not in prison. I'm sure we could break whatever code they're using for communications to the outside, but it would take time."

"Good idea, Duncan, but you're right. It would take time."

"Any way to take him out of the prison? Or transfer him?" asked Mary O'Reilly. "It would be easier then."

"He's lawyered up. And California law is liberal when it comes to prisoner's rights. No chance of touching him legally."

"It's really quite simple," Kamon announced quietly. "MAC wants to know his thoughts. Correct? And what he has planned. Right? I can get that information. I'll go. What good is it to be a Native American Mind Walker if I can't use it?"

"I thought of you Kamon, but you're the war commander, my second in command. If anything happens, you're needed here. And you know how dangerous it is for you to Walk through mentally deranged minds. Make no mistake this guy is psychotic and unbelievably unbalanced. And mentally strong. I don't dare See him as he's too unstable. There could be a possibility of being trapped inside his derangement."

Kamon addressed Catherine as if she was the only one in the room. "You also know the rules for each of us whom much has been given. We must use it to help. And Catherine, I choose. My choice. The valley is secure. Trent is here in Shadow Valley as your bodyguard, as well as the entire Sgnoch Council. Both Brenna and Raina are protected by trained Warriors although that damn Raina...," he let his voice drift off.

"Anyway Catherine, there is no threat to you that we know of right now. I'm going. End of story." He looked intently at Catherine, wanting her to understand. "Please give me your permission, or at least say that I have your blessing. Now, do you have a need for me to be at the rest of this meeting because it seems that time may be of the essence."

"You do choose, Kamon. And you know that you have my approval and appreciation. I will worry, however. You know how to contact MAC. Please be safe," Catherine said as Kamon strode quickly out with a faint nod of thanks in her direction. He didn't even glance at anyone else, knowing that his decision could impact everyone's future.

"I have only a vague idea of what MAC is," commented Robert Neal, interrupting Catherine's thoughts. A cousin of Kamon and Kelly Pierce's, he had been away from the Shadow Valley most of his adult life. A family situation and the death of an unborn child had left him desolate, he had come home to the valley to heal.

Brenna had teased Catherine when she appointed him as a temporary replacement for Kelly Pierce that she just liked to look at the very handsome face. More than six feet two of calm, with the golden-brown skin of a mixed race, he had black eyes, sculptured face, and wide shoulders. His straight pale blond hair completed the picture of a stunning man.

"MAC is men from various walks of life who act as volunteer enforcers in situations where the country's laws cannot, or has not, been observed. They are not all Scots, but of many races. Men who have been specially trained as elite warriors. I'm not sure what the letters MAC stand for."

"Daintily put. Bob, they are Swords when one is needed. Silent, strong, menacing weapons," stated Mr. MacPherson firmly, his dark eyes unwavering from the other man's.

"Shields and Swords. Of course, that makes sense," murmured Neal referring to the ageless vow. "And that damn Raina remark?"

Catherine grinned. "Bob, you're new to Council, so let me fill in some details and bring your knowledge of this Council up to speed. As far as I know MAC stands for nothing, but Mac often meant the son of in Scotland. It may be an abbreviation for something else, even in Gaelic, but I don't know it".

She smiled, continuing, "As for the other, suffice it to say that Raina and Kamon have an involved history. At the moment

Raina and Sean McKinney, identical twin to Liam, have gone awanderin' as they called it to see other places. They left with my permission, but didn't tell anyone else they were going, including Kamon who has acted as Raina's bodyguard for years. They joined Brenna and Deke for a short time at the last disaster site from that tornado in Oklahoma. The last I heard, a week ago, they were having a wonderful time exploring different States and learning about other people."

"Seems Kamon is more involved than he is not," mused Neal with a slight smile.

"That's the right of it," grinned Duncan Frasier. Smiles were exchanged around the table.

As soon as the meeting finished, Catherine called Brenna to fill her in to the new developments concerning MAC. "Good evening, sister of mine."

"Hey Catherine," said Brenna fighting through a huge yawn. "Sorry, I wasn't available when you called earlier, but all I can do is sleep. And more sleep. Deke and Brandon are joined at the hip thank goodness, and as long as they have horses they're both happy."

"Yeah, but all this sleeping is just for a short time and then we get a baby out of it. Thank goodness, I'm over that stage. The Sgnoch Council met this morning." Catherine then proceeded to relate all the points of the meeting ending with Bob's comments about Kamon and Raina.

"Catherine, before we move on to another problem, where exactly in California is Kamon headed? To what prison?" asked Brenna, nibbling on her bottom lip.

"A small maximum-security prison halfway between the coast and the Sierra Mountains called Sanmore Prison. It's isolated, but there's a little town nearby named Leddic. Why? Is it important?"

"I talked to Sean and Raina last night. I meant to call you afterward but I fell asleep. I'm sorry, Catherine but …."

"Anything wrong?" Catherine interrupted.

"There was an earthquake day before yesterday in Leddic,

California. One person dead, dozens injured. I got a call from a FEMA government man requesting help, especially from Raina and Sean. They did too good a job as volunteers at the disaster site in Oklahoma. Deke absolutely forbids me to go further than the front door of the ranch house which doesn't bother me as all I can do is sleep. Anyway, Raina and Sean are on their way to California. They planned to drive all night, and expected to be in Leddic early this morning. Mr. Horton didn't mention damage to a prison."

"I'll call Kamon and tell him about the earthquake which may have affected the prison. I will not tell him the whereabouts of Raina and Sean. They may or may not run into each other. As Destiny chooses."

CHAPTER TEN

Kamon Youngblood sat in the wooden chair facing the steel wire and glass grid separating the visitors from the prisoners. The room was empty except for two armed guards, one at the side of the room and the other guarding the entry door, the only way in or out. There had been an earthquake in the area where the prison was situated, but the prison buildings were newly built and little damage was done.

He had spent the last several days being briefed on the horrific crimes that the prisoner, Matteus, had committed, sickening incidents but necessary to know for this meeting. He had interviewed half a dozen men on the same cell-block as Matteus since his arrival. MAC had arranged for journalist credentials under the name of Jess Wolfe, and a cover story of interviewing prisoners for rumored mistreatments by the prison guards.

The men he had interviewed always could remember some alleged abuse that the guards had done to them. Kamon carefully wrote down their stories, seeming fascinated and wide-eyed at the ill-treatment, assuring each prisoner that his story would get back to the appropriate authorities. And it would. A copy of the tape wired to his body with the warden's permission would be given to the administration to review. What they wouldn't get was the information he would obtain secretly.

The next man who entered was massive. Standing about six foot six or so, with huge arms and legs, and a chest like an oak tree trunk. His large face had a peculiar prettiness to it. Fine honed features with long curling eye lashes, totally at odds with the immense body covered with dark tattoos. Particularly fascinating and disconcerting was the tattooed snake crawling up his neck and into his ear.

"You the writer?" asked the huge man. Without waiting for an answer he said, "My name is Matteus, but they call me El Jefe, the boss." His face was expressionless.

"I'm Jess Wolfe, from the New York Examiner," Kamon lied. "My editor heard that some of the prisoners here have been mistreated by some of the guards. He wanted me to do a follow-up story."

"Yeah, this prison sucks. The guards rough you up for no reason. Sadistic behavior. I think they chose the guards here that couldn't get no other jobs." He continued talking in the same vein, with curse words mixed into every sentence. He began to tell a long rambling story about going to the prison hospital after he had been in a fight, and how they refused to take him to an outside hospital.

Kamon was grateful that Grandfather Youngblood had insisted that he study all the known elements of the brain, and commit them to memory. Knowing that the brain had two halves, almost identical in size but with some difference in usages and that they were separated by a much traveled bridge-way was helpful to transverse the intricacies of the inner brain.

His goal in Mind Walking with this particular subject was to quickly gain access to memories, knowing that memories are cloned and stored in many parts of the brain but mostly in the hippocampus. Sometimes the stimulus of Mind Walking triggered a multi-media reaction which allowed a visual past to be quickly observable. Kamon knew that the occipital lobe was located near the back of the head where visual images were processed. His plan in Walking through this man's brain was to enter through the eyes, then traverse directly into the occipital lobe located at the back of the head, and search for visual areas that had been processed. He hoped that this man's brain would be a quick Walk.

Kamon concentrated looking into Matteus's eyes as he slowly entered into the man's mind. The jolt was painful with its intensity. During his years as an interrogator in covert operations, and later with MAC, he had entered some really bad people's minds; psychotics, fanatics, and the barely sane. Soldiers who were numb from killing as ordered. This man was different from all of those.

This man was truly evil.

Bracing himself mentally for the coming onslaught of images, he took a deep cleansing breath and separated himself from what he would find. Analyzing the memories and all the data obtained would come only after the session was finished. For now, he had to simply accept all the information he could find.

He continued to maintain eye contact with Matteus as if he was listening to the spewing diatribe the man had against the prison authorities. All he could do was shake his head in agreement as if all the lies were in fact truths, as part of his own mind delved into Matteus's. Note taking was impossible. It took all his concentration to separate Walking through Matteus's brain and maintaining the image of listening.

Matteus's brain was a living nightmare. All people's brains are a complicated inter-connected system with linkages to all other parts through various pathways. Matteus's brain had arrested bleeding, healed lesions, and scar tissue all making the major pathways difficult to navigate. It was like a maze where the pattern was disrupted making the openings twisted. And very scarred.

Kamon's Walking moved like smoke through the tissue of the Occipital lobe of Matteus's brain, seeing objects, words, faces and color. He moved on to the left temporal lobe collecting images as he went as he knew that long-term memories involving people and animals were often associated with the anterior-temporal lobe, but objects tended to be stored in the left temporal-occipital lobe.

Bingo. Kamon felt a flood of memories and emotions coming from the area where speech comprehension, sound and some memory normally resided. At the same time, he felt sick to his stomach and wanted to retch. Whatever he was seeing and feeling was making him physically ill. He slowly moved back to

Matteus's eyes then out, separating himself from Mind Walking. He lifted his left shoulder slightly signaling the inside guard that he needed to leave.

"Your times up," the guard said, tapping Kamon heavily on the shoulder.

"Hey, I wasn't finished talking, you stupid pig," protested Matteus, standing to his full height, making himself as large and intimidating as possible.

"Tough," pronounced the short heavy-set guard. "His time is up."

"Maybe I can come back," Kamon said hoping to deter any violence. "Thanks for seeing me. I'll file all you told me with my editor."

He quickly followed the guard out, walking through a maze of large and small rooms before leaving the building. They went through several checkpoints with guards carrying guns before finally reaching the outside. The guard who had been inside with him moved silently beside him until they reached a black SUV parked in front of the prison gates. Kamon opened the back door and got in beside a larger man. The guard got in beside him. Another man drove the SUV.

"Let me rest for a moment," Kamon said, closing his eyes to ward off the nausea. "Better yet, roll down the windows and make sure I have a barf bag. And I'm not kidding," he said quietly leaning his head back against the seat.

The car moved quickly down the highway, the wind blowing into all the opened windows. A plastic bag was put into Kamon's hands.

"Damn," said Kamon softly taking deep breaths seeking to calm his stomach. "Okay. I'm okay for now."

"Sorry," said the large younger man. "Do you need more time?" At Kamon's negative nod he said, "For now you can call me Sam. This is" he hesitated, "Jim," as he pointed to the man who had acted as guard. "Our driver is John."

"Kamon. Kamon Youngblood. How much of the information do you want?"

"Whatever you think is pertinent that we can use."

Kamon closed his eyes to focus, and reconnect with his inner being. He answered in a low voice, "Matteus is insane, and the Devil incarnate. Depraved. Without conscience. Immoral. A psychopath."

"Explain the word psychopath. I'm not sure of all the meanings," said Jim.

"The short answer is a person emotionally cold, a lack of remorse and a love of risk taking. The scientific explanation is that it is thought that the part of the brain, the amygdale, malfunctions particularly in the right hemisphere. There is little response at the sign of another person's distress and there is no reaction to threats."

"Then consequences are useless?"

"Essentially, yes. Psychopaths are immune to remorse and punishment. Lots of theories why psychopathic behaviors exist. In Matteus's case, he was beaten and abused both physically and sexually from the time he was born. I only entered a small portion of his brain and it was a mass of twisted pathways. He has been beaten on the head more times than even he remembers."

Kamon continued, his eyes closed. "He is a pedophile with a penchant for preadolescent girls or boys, but preferably girls. He gets off on torturing his victims sexually before killing them. His memories are of stuffing objects into any bodily opening before their death. He enjoys killing; grown men, little girls, women, whoever, even animals, preferably with a butcher knife."

"Good God," breathed John from the front seat.

The other man, Sam, simply asked, "How does this fit into virtually kidnapping all those little girls. He certainly can't physically touch them."

"I don't know for sure. His brain is such a maze that some of the connections are dead-ended. The frontal lobe of the brain is where the executive functions occur; the thinking, planning, conceptualizing plus the appreciation of emotion. I didn't go there. I don't know if I can and I sure to hell don't want to. I found out that the girls are going to be taken on the first of the month to a camp near Guaymus, Mexico. I can draw you a map of the area where the camp is."

"Would you mind if I asked you a question about your Mind Walking?" asked Sam, the obvious leader of the group.

"Ask. I may not answer however."

"If you were in a space, for want of a better word, of long-term memories …?"

"How could I access the area of the camp where this will take place? Because it was in Matteus's long term memory bank. This all has happened before."

All the men remained quiet for a couple of minutes processing the knowledge.

"Then we need to immediately erase these so-called humans from the face of the earth," Sam said quietly without emotion. "Our first priority will be the men who will take the girls from their homes."

"How do you plan on handling that without an international incident with the Mexican government? Their hands may be clean, but a group of men coming into their country and killing people will not go over well. It may also not be acceptable to our own government," said Jim cautiously.

"Then its best that they don't know, isn't it?" the leader said coldly. "My men will transfer the men sent to pick up the girl children to a ship in international waters. That's worked very well before. What happens to the men afterward will depend on their involvement in the scheme, and to what, or whom, they owe their allegiance."

"I don't really give a damn about what happens to the men," Kamon retorted sharply. "But the families are very poor people with little to no education. How are you going to handle the girls and their families who have been promised a luxurious childhood vacation? You're going to have some very disappointed, angry people. They have no clue to the real purpose of the trip nor the dangers involved. Complaints could be noisy and attention getting."

"And they will get something even better. There is an Aid group in place that helps families at risk financially until children are eighteen years of age. We can add monies for social workers, career advisors, and anything else we can think of. We can run the project through Students for A Better Life, a subsidy of an International Aid Organization very much like the one your cousin works for."

"May I ask a question?" queried Kamon, lifting an eyebrow in question.

"Ask. I may not answer," said Sam, repeating Kamon's words back to him.

"Do you work with MAC all the time? Either of you?"

Sam answered first, "No. Only when my particular skills are needed."

"And your skills are?"

Silence.

Jim broke the silence. "I don't work for MAC. I'm a liaison officer working for an initialed agency of the United States. The government's interests are in a potential prison break. We don't have access to people like you ourselves."

"And you still don't," Sam replied. "The promise was made that how we got the information would drop into a deep dark hole. If there is leakage in any manner, we told your agency of the consequences for all the people involved. You knew this personally, Jim, before you took this assignment. And John, our driver, is with me. MAC and its resources will stay top secret and clandestine forevermore. There is an old Scottish saying, 'The penalty for betrayal is death'."

Jim nodded in agreement, his hands trembling slightly.

"Changing the subject, I'd like to go into Mexico with you. I may be of some help. As a Native American, I can pass as Mexican and I'm fluent in the language."

"You have that right," Sam agreed. "Jim?"

"Hell yes. This little bald-headed Irishman hates predators of all kinds, especially those who prey on children. I'm in. And forevermore," he agreed alluding to keeping Kamon's abilities confidential.

CHAPTER ELEVEN

"Earthquakes are too similar to tornados," commented Raina to Mr. Horton, the FEMA representative they had known in Oklahoma. "The destruction to buildings is similar, but the debris field is not as wide spread. Deeper rubble though, heavy equipment is really going to be needed here. Do you have more volunteers that can operate bulldozers?"

"I'm not sure. Washington sent me here temporarily. And they are sending out a crew and an experienced manager from Washington the first of next week. I do have some men coming in this afternoon from a construction site. The state is loaning them to us for a couple of weeks if we need them. There're volunteers, both local and throughout the state, but I don't know their skills. What do you think is the best way for me to start on this one? I've never handled an earthquake site."

Raina hid her smile noting the me and I in his sentence. Government officials were always protecting their backsides. As far as she could see politics was just ugly. Half the time they couldn't be productive for other people, because their hands were full protecting themselves.

"I suggest that we have each volunteer fill out those sheets we made up in Oklahoma." At his blank look, she added "The one's that gives you all the information and the skills that each volunteer has. Then you can divide the groups up into teams, choosing people's strengths to fit the site they're to work on."

He leaned forward, listening intently as if he was taking notes.

"For instance, that dark-haired lady is tiny, but I have talked to her and she is detailed oriented. I'd assign her as a team leader to pick through the site to gather up any mementos or anything else that could be salvaged. Her attention to minutia will help other people focus on small objects." Raina continued, pointing to a couple of men, "Those two people over there look like they could handle heavier lifting, so I'd suggest you assign them to picking through those large boxes on the edge of that platform. I also suggest that you choose block leaders to facilitate sectioning off each site for maximum benefits."

"Excellent! Excellent! I'll do just that. Anna, come with me so that you can organize them into their groups. Shane, come with us so you'll know where the heavy equipment is needed. There are hired crews besides the volunteers so you can sort that all out."

Raina gave Sean a wide grin. They had made a bet as to how long it would take for Mr. Horton to put someone else in charge. She had said within the hour, Sean said no more than fifteen minutes. Sean had won, of course.

"Anna, some of the medical students from Stanford have promised to come down and help with clean-up when they're not needed for the injured. Keep an eye out for them, please. Put them wherever you need them most without getting them hurt."

"Sure, what ever you say, boss man," said Raina with a hint of aspersion in her voice. "You do realize that Shane and I are volunteers and I hate taking orders."

"I'm sorry. I'm sorry. It's that you look so young, but you give orders like a four-star. I was in the Army and my General was the best in the service. Anna, whatever you do to help is really appreciated. I offered to put you on the payroll but you refused in Oklahoma. Do you need to be paid? It's not much, but it would help with your and Shane's expenses," he added looking at Raina's clean but well-worn clothes. Sean's shirt and jeans weren't in any better shape than hers.

"We're okay for now," replied Sean. "Paperwork is a pain." In an aside he whispered to Raina, as Mr. Horton walked away. "And leaves a permanent computer trail to follow. Which we absolutely do not need."

Buying clothes was not a priority for either of them. They visited a Laundromat regularly, but neat, clean, and simple were the operative words. And to fit in so as not to capture anyone's notice. Their work clothes had come mostly from thrift stores.

"It's time for our weekly call to Catherine. Are you going to tell her or do I have to? I will if you don't," Sean threatened. "She has to know. Neither of us is willing to face an angry leader."

Glaring at him, Raina sighed. "You tell her, then I'll talk to her because I know she'll have questions that I can't answer."

Dialing the phone, he said, "Catherine, we're in California at the earthquake site that Brenna told you we were going. Yeah. That's not what I called for. It's Raina. She's been having what she calls dreams. Dreams of horrific events like major nightmares. I leave the door open between our rooms so I can hear her. She seemed to be mumbling words, but nothing that makes sense, least that I could understand. Then today, we were sitting resting on a slab of concrete, and she closed her eyes and told me some hair-raising story about abused children somewhere. She says she didn't know them, nor had any other episodes like this."

"I'm not sure what's happening. Was she upset by her dream-in-day? What was her mood?" asked Catherine.

"That's another odd part. At first it was like an ordinary nightmare, you know the kind where monsters are hiding out in the closet. Today, she was wide awake kind of staring into space, and still saw stuff. She isn't upset by it, seems to take it for granted. Frankly, it scared the shit out of me. Sorry for the language but it does make my point."

"Grandmother Ramsey and Grandfather Youngblood told me years ago that Raina was very sensitive to feelings of others. And she had many talents as she had probably run from line to line before her birth to gathered as many as was possible to hold. It was only a half-joke. We've always known that she could organize a third-world country. Put Raina on the phone."

"Catherine, Sean is upset over what I told him."

"I take it that you're not upset?" asked Catherine in a soft, calm voice.

"No, I'm not. Catherine, it seemed normal to me. I saw terrible things, but it's like I'm removed from them. Like a third person. An observer, like a movie. Today's frightening dream or whatever, happened in a blink of an eye. Since I don't know if this is my very fertile imagination, or if somehow I'm picking up something else, I have no way of knowing how true my dreams-in-day are. It's strange, but my feelings aren't involved and you know that emotions are at the center of my being. Am I making sense at all?"

"Describe to me what you saw Raina. Did you not see people?"

"I only see children from a distance, but somehow I know they are frightened, and I know that they have been hurt. I don't see them getting hurt, but I know they have been. I wanted to try to concentrate, to focus in on the dream-in-day to see what would happen, but Sean said I had to talk to you first."

"Sean's job is to protect you. His call was right, Raina. Until you are in a controlled environment like here in Shadow Valley, you may not experiment. If you have any other nightmares, or even dreams in the day time, call me immediately. Do you understand? I don't know the extent of this new development, so we're going to play it safe. Agreed?"

"Of course, Catherine. I don't feel odd about it though. It happens suddenly and stays with me for a minute or so. It's like a brief glimpse of a television movie trailer is the best way I could describe it. Like it makes a little sense, but not much."

"I don't know exactly what is happening. Right now it would be an educated guess on my part. Since you don't feel a personal involvement I think it is a wait and see endeavor. Remember Grandfather said that all things were alive in nature, every rock, tree, or object and nothing truly fades away permanently. Basically, are you feeling any different? Headaches? Nausea?"

"That makes sense, sort of. I do have a headache sometimes, but it's very sporadic, mostly in the afternoons, but it could be from the sun."

"Or stress. Brenna says that Mr. Horton places a lot of responsibility on you."

"And I love it. It's really nice to be needed. And Mr. Horton is caring, but clueless to practicalities. He is fabulous about paperwork though. I actually like to work for him. I think we make a good team, along with Sean's heavy lifting."

"That's because he lets you do everything your way," kidded Sean in the background.

"True. But he does think most of it is his idea."

"Do you two need to come home?"

Raina and Sean looked at each other in horror and said "No," at the same time.

Sean added, "No! Please no. If there is a problem, or if I considered Raina to be unsafe in any way, I promise you we'll be on the first flight home. Catherine, this has been the best trip of our lives. We've learned so much in the last several months. Not only about our wonderful diverse country, but about ourselves. We've met so many people living so many different lives from the one we are familiar with. It was a good idea for us to be part of the work force. It gave us a different perspective than just talking with people. And we've maybe even grown up a little. Being responsible for ourselves and helping clean up areas of disasters is a turn-on, I don't know how to say it any other way."

"Okay, but call me if you need me, day or night. Or if anything different crops up."

They promised immediately. Neither of them would take a chance of disobeying Catherine.

CHAPTER TWELVE

"**A**h Hell!" Kamon said in disgust. "I don't need this. I don't even know if I can. Matteus's brain is a mass of messed up tissue. And that particular part of the brain may be completely gone, or at least not accessible."

Sam sat watching quietly, waiting for Kamon's decision.

On the first of the month, the men who were posing as the young girl's bus drivers were spirited away, unseen by the girls or their families. Instead a battalion of Spanish-speaking social workers met each family and apologized for the camp closing due to financial problems. Since that was a common cry throughout the poor country no undue questions were asked.

Instead the assigned social workers said that an International Students for A Better Life Organization would help with the girl's school expenses based on family need. The parents were delighted with the new development as the aid organization would also help to provide food for the family. Each family would be assessed separately, and then the on-going process would be monitored by the local priest and a social worker. Job training would also be available for parents when needed. The training would also include basic education classes in Spanish as many parents and children could not read or write.

The interrogation of the men did not turn out so well. A couple of the men were not involved in any covert activity, and had been hired because they could drive a bus. Several others however were criminals with gang affiliations, and a history of violence. The latter simply disappeared from the ship. Jim said he was told that they would be imprisoned in another Latin country. Whether that was a lie or not was anyone's guess.

Kamon didn't ask any questions. He didn't want to know. And truthfully, he did not care. People chose much of their own fate, and consequences could be hell.

One very cocky young gangster told the interrogator that they would do as they pleased, and the United States with their weak laws couldn't stop them. He also bragged that a major assault was planned on a Southern California mall as soon as El Jefe joined them. The interrogator asked Sam to join him in talking to the man. Before any further questioning could be done, one of the other men had jumped forward and snapped the young gangster's neck.

"We don't know if the little bastard was even telling the truth. He was probably blowing smoke just to confuse us," stated Kamon, pacing the room.

Sam remained silent, his arms folded across his chest. The decision was Kamon's.

"If he was telling the truth, then there must be a prison break planned, and a gang invasion of a mall. A mall where hundreds of innocent people could be killed. Crap! He might have been as crazy as Matteus. But if he is accurate then we need to know it, and take measures to stop it. The quickest way is for me to go back and search Matteus's mind."

"We will do whatever you decide. Kamon, that is the quickest way, but not the only way. The reality is that we're back to not knowing the timing for any of this. We might have time to beef up the security ...."

"And you might not. And all hell might break loose."

Sam didn't bother to deny the reality.

"I have to go back. If I can find a way to check the frontal area of the brain it will tell me Matteus's thinking and planning ... you can fit me with a wire. That way no matter what happens you will have some information. My vow is To Serve. I may never know your real name, but I'm positive your motto is the same as mine. To Serve. To act as Sword and Shield."

Sam gave a slight nod of his head.

Kamon didn't tell Sam of the possible dangers of linking

with the criminally insane. Mind Walking was an ancient form of telepathy, and was closely tied to intense emotions. There was also a biological connection between the people connected with brain waves changing to match the sender's. Scary stuff considering that he already knew that Matteus's mind was verging on insanity. Exchanging the time of day would have been daunting, but processing the exchange of information from Matteus's brain was downright terrifying. He reminded himself of his oath. To Serve. Sword and Shield.

"Okay, let's do this."

Kamon went through the same process as before, letting all the prisoners know that he was back to continue the investigation of prison abuse. He interviewed several men, then finally called Matteus.

"You're back. I didn't think you'd come back. I got a lot more to tell you about these damn guards. You look Mexican, do you speak it?"

"Si," answered Kamon.

"In English," demanded the heavy-set guard inside the barricade. Another guard, Jim, had returned to his original post of outside barricade protection for Kamon. Matteus's glare didn't affect either guard in the least.

"I think better in Spanish, you uneducated pig," protested Matteus. "You're afraid I'll tell him all the dirt on this prison. That there's harassment and guard brutality."

Neither guard even glanced at the prisoner.

"In English then," said Kamon slowly. "I know you wanted to tell me about the conditions of the cell units."

"Ugh, yeah," Matteus squinted his eyes to organize his thoughts. When he opened them wider he put his hand to his left temple.

"A problem," asked Kamon softly. "Headache?"

"Ah, pain. It's nothing. I don't let any shit like that bother me. Pain means nothing to me."

Kamon had entered Matteus's brain when he had widened his eyes. Now he drifted toward the frontal section of the brain, carefully working through sections, often detouring when a pathway was blocked by scar tissue.

As Kamon mind traveled to the frontal area of Matteus's brain, extreme anger overlaid everything. The normal communication between the amygdala and the frontal lobes had reduced neural activity which in turn left little communication as a balance between reason and emotion. The normal restraints over Matteus's rage-filled behavior were missing, leaving only deep overwhelming anger and making Kamon gasp silently in physical pain. Kamon breathed deeply seeking to lower his own heartbeat and enhance his body control. He focused instead on the front part of Matteus's brain above his eyes. The area was a mass of mangled scarred flesh, and was difficult to filter or wade through.

Suddenly Matteus gave off a wave of hatred tinged with intense fear engulfing Kamon's being. The strong emotions physically shocked Kamon as if he had been hit with a high voltage electric wire. He felt himself falling from the chair as blackness rose to claim him. He knew he was losing consciousness, that somehow he had failed. Throwing his head back he tried to dislodge his connections from Matteus and yelled as loud as he was able. "Lies. They were all lies," and then his world went blank.

"A Brujo," shouted Matteus. "A Witch. The Sorcerer came for me. Help. Help. He's stealing me. Don't let him take me." He began to babble incoherently in a mix of Spanish and English. "The Cunandero's said the devils would eat my soul. Now he's come. The devil is in my brain. Out. Out. Get out!" he screamed as if in agony holding his head in his hands.

His agitation increased as he fell into complete madness, shouting and pushing the inside guards. An alarm sounded bringing more guards to help subdue the gigantic prisoner, which brought more chaos to the room. Matteus picked up a chair and threw it at the unbreakable plate glass window, and then turned the full rage of his delusions toward the guards. Several tasers had to be used to finally subdue the now babbling, frothing-at-the-mouth prisoner. Matteus was now completely insane.

Using the confusion as a screen, Jim picked up the unconscious Kamon in his arms. He hurried back through the maze of rooms and was doubly grateful that he had arranged for two extra uniformed guards waiting just outside the visitor door. The largest guard took Kamon from Jim, and carried him over his shoulder, fireman's style. The warden had shifted special guards to facilitate the MAC group as he hoped to gain need information on any future problems. Now the guards led the small group through the buildings as rapidly as they could move. The trio carrying Kamon exited through a side gate to the waiting car. The largest guard put Kamon onto the back seat, gave a slight salute to Jim, and the two men jogged back into the prison.

At Sam's raised eyebrow, Jim murmured, "Once a Marine, always a Marine. I thought I might need a little help, so I checked on some people I knew was here."

"What happened in there? Kamon's breathing, but he's unconscious."

"I haven't the vaguest. Everything seemed normal. I heard Kamon say 'lies, they were all lies' before he passed out.

"Did something else happen? Was he hit? Why is he unconscious?"

"Nothing happened. At least nothing seemed to happen. Kamon was listening to Matteus's ravings, and suddenly he slumped over and passed out. Matteus was shouting things like Brujo and Witch and then he went berserk. Completely crazy, foaming-at-the-mouth insane. Matteus was fighting the guards and throwing chairs, they were having a difficult time getting him under control. I got Kamon out while everyone was focused on Matteus with a little help from friends."

"That was best. And now we know they were lies and there is no impeding prison break. I have to call MAC's friends to ask what they want us to do now with an unconscious Kamon. For now, lay him on the back seat, and cover him with blankets in case he's in shock. Hell, I don't know what else to do. Take him to the hospital, what?" he asked a silent Jim.

Using his cell phone, he dialed a number. "Hello, this is a MAC operative. We are at the prison near Leddic, California. Kamon Youngblood was in the processing of obtaining information from a prisoner when he suddenly slumped over, and became unconscious. He's breathing okay, and there doesn't seem to be any injuries, but he's out cold. Yes. We are outside the Sanmore prison now, and he's lying in the back seat of the car. I don't know, nothing seems to have happened. I'm putting you on speaker phone so my two companions can also hear.

"Do you want us to take him to the nearest hospital, or have the doctors on staff here take a look at him?"

"Neither" came a hard firm voice. "No, definitely not. The first thing they would do is an MRI, and that can't happen. What's the closest airport that will take a jet?"

"I know the Monterrey airport would, not sure about the others in the area. It's about a thirty-five-minute drive I think. Maybe closer."

"Take him there. To the private airplane section, we'll clear you from here. Wait there and someone will pick Kamon up in a small jet," said the disembodied voice. "Do not interact with anyone. Do you understand? No one must see him. You three are the only people who know and have seen Kamon's abilities. Tell MAC we will personally deal with any repercussions if the vow of silence is broken. All of you knew the penalty for betrayal before you took this assignment."

The line went dead.

"Holy shit," breathed Jim shuddering. "If that wasn't a promised threat I don't know what it was."

"I couldn't have said it better myself. Now you realize that talking about this episode, for want of a better word to anyone would be fatal. Their rule is strictly enforced and applies to everyone, no matter what your title."

"To my grave," vowed Jim fervently. "Forevermore. Quite literally."

"Amen," said Sam and John together.

CHAPTER THIRTEEN

"Sean?"

"Hey Catherine, I was just going to call you. We're ..."

"Sean, stop. Where are you? Is Raina with you?"

"Yes, she's asleep now, but she's sick. We're in the car driving from Monterrey. We left the Monterrey Aquarium where we were sightseeing about a half hour ago. We are on our way to San Francisco."

"How sick is she?" Catherine interrupted.

"I don't know exactly," admitted Sean. "We were watching a pod of dolphins play outside the aquarium when she said she had a headache. She complained of feeling nauseous and light-headed. She got in the car, but then vomited. I was calling you to tell you that I think she should be seen by a doctor. She may have picked up some sort of bug from the earthquake site. She's in the backseat sleeping now."

"I'm sorry, but you're going to have to wake her up. I need to know how ill my baby sister is. And put this on encrypted speaker phone."

"Okay, I'll pull off the road." He pulled into a nearby turn-out. "Raina, wake up." Sean shook her arm. "Come on Raina, Catherine wants to talk to you."

"Stop. Don't shake me. My head hurts," she moaned. "Catherine?"

"Raina, Sean. There's no easy way to say this. Listen carefully. Kamon was getting some information from the mind of a prisoner at Sanmore Prison there in California, near Leddic. During an interview, he fell unconscious and we don't know why. We don't know if he was connected to a prisoner, or if he is ill with something else. He spent some time in Mexico recently."

"Liam was at Lockheed in California working on that new drone. He's borrowing one of their planes, and is on his way to pick him up at the Monterrey Airport. I've asked Deke for permission to have Brenna treat him at their Texas ranch. I need you to meet Liam. A quick EMT assessment, please. We can decide what to do then. How are you feeling now, Raina?"

"I had a short nap. I feel better I think. Still a little woozy and a little remaining headache," replied Raina, slowly moving her head from side to side to test for residual pain.

"Brenna's not coming out?" asked Sean as he proceeded to make a U-turn back toward Monterrey.

"No, I've chosen not to tell her yet. Her pregnancy is not doing well right now, that's why I went through Deke. Besides, she couldn't assess Kamon's brain without possibly harming her unborn. She's going to be pissed, as you would say, Raina, but I don't need to argue with her either. I'll tell her next, and that I want to send you all to Texas where she is."

"We left the Leddic area yesterday. We didn't even know that there was a prison there," stated Sean bluntly.

"We were too busy doing our own jobs, Sean. Catherine, I was an idiot. Running didn't solve much. I'm sorry you've had to do everything these last few months. I should have stayed to help you. Although we've learned an enormous amount."

"No, you needed this time out of time to broaden yourself. You and Sean. There's an SUV bringing Kamon to the airport, part of a collaboration with MAC. The car should be big and black. Please guard your identities, people at the earthquake site know who you supposedly are, but no one else."

"As I told you before, the only person who knows our true identity is Eric Shirt, Dr. Farrison's grandson, who is a medical student at Stanford. He helped at the earthquake site. He knew about parts of Shadow Valley already, and he knows that we were awanderin' incognito. We can talk about him when we get back, but he will not discuss us with anyone. Okay, at the airport we'll either board first, or wait until the other people leave, depending on their arrival time. Is that okay?' asked Sean.

"Yes, I'll call a representative from MAC to pick up your car. Just leave the keys under the passenger seat."

"All right. Is everything else okay? Are you?" asked Raina, as she became more alert.

"I'm fine. Raina. And the pain in your head, a massive headache you said? Maybe ...," Catherine's voice drifted off as she murmured softly, "As the Creator chooses. Call me from the plane," she asserted as she hung up.

Raina swiped at the tears running down her face. Hearing that Kamon was unconscious had made her heart stop. Nothing could go wrong with him. He was invincible, untouchable, the strongest man she knew in spirit and in mind. He would hate to be unconscious and unaware of his surroundings, but he would detest being dependent on other people more.

Control was Kamon's mainstay. Control of all his faculties, mind, emotions and body. One of the many reasons she had so loved to tease him. That instant when his self-imposed restraint slipped left his heart open. She had lived for those moments.

Looking back, it had been a selfish act on her part. She had no right to force what she wanted on him. She knew that he had been unable to block her from his mind, and she had taken advantage of that. Now she was sorry for her unwanted, vain behavior. Unless the heart is given freely, emotions are only stolen moments. One of the many lessons she had learned since leaving home.

Sean and Raina reached the airport before Liam's plane arrived, but a large black SUV sat alone on a distance tarmac. Sean parked near enough to watch the SUV, but not close enough to be detected. Both watched in silence, lost in their own thoughts.

About twenty minutes later, a little private jet landed, taxing close to the black SUV. Three men exited the SUV, two men carrying the limp body of Kamon. The car's driver carried a large duffel bag and a metal case. The three men were only in the airplane for a couple of minutes before exiting, and hurrying toward their car.

Sean and Raina watched as the large SUV drove through the gates, and then into airport traffic. They jogged over to the airplane and boarded with their beat up suitcases and a couple of canvas bags. A brief greeting with Liam, and the plane was back in the air.

"Raina, call Brenna and Catherine with the airplane speaker phone, and then help me here," Sean requested.

Raina silently followed Sean's instructions, connecting with both her sisters by speaker phone.

"Brenna? Sean. I'm checking Kamon's vital signs now. No airway instability, breathing a little rapid. Blood pressure a little high, pulse weak and erratic. Temperature below normal. No dilation of pupils." He stripped Kamon of clothes, checking for any sign of damage from an invasive instrument like a needle or a puncture wound. "There are no signs of trauma on any part of Kamon's body, nor any puncture wounds."

Brenna's voice came over the phone. "It doesn't sound like anything physical like a stroke, cardiac infarc, seizure, or any other anoxia or ischemia. It sounds more like a reaction that is in direct relationship with the prisoner he was with. Opening another's mind is a two-way street. We don't know how long the connection between them lasted, or the intensity involved, nor what he saw. The unconsciousness or coma can be in direct proportion to the duration of the exposure. Or it could be…," her voice drifted off. "Never mind, right now it's all guess work. Just maintenance now, please."

"Nothing we can do right now? I put him in a pair of sterile scrubs, I didn't want to put him in any of his own clothes in case of contamination. And I've covered him with a couple of blankets to keep him warm but …," Sean let his voice deliberately cut off with uncertainty.

"There's nothing more you can do right now, just continue to treat him for shock. No fluids, nothing until he's here. What's your gut reaction, Sean?"

Sean was silent for a moment, and then said, "I don't know

Brenna, but to me it looks more like an electrical shock, or maybe complete exhaustion, or both."

"Raina? What does it feel like to you, not what you see?"

"I'm not the best judge right now, I got some food poisoning or something, and have a pounding headache and nausea. I do agree with Sean though. Kamon's pale, but he doesn't feel critical to me."

"Catherine?" asked Brenna.

"Maybe. Strange things are."

"What does that mean Catherine?" asked Sean. "Maybe, strange what?"

"Never mind for now. It means that supportive care is the best we can do until you get here. See you in Texas," said Brenna briskly as she hung up.

Raina and Sean stood watch over Kamon, but he remained silent and unresponsive. Sean finally moved up to the cockpit to act as copilot for his twin, and perhaps patch up some hurt feelings caused from his own abrupt leaving and lack of contact.

Raina was silent as she focused on the man who had been her biggest dream, and influenced the most emotional reactions in her life. Even now, pale and ill, she was taken back by how physically beautiful a man he was. When she was near him, his intensity was overwhelming, sending off waves of reactions. This was the man she had wanted to please above all others. Her hand moved toward his face before she brought herself back under control. It wasn't her right to touch him when he had no decision in the process.

Instead of her hand, she allowed her eyes to run slowly over the two thin scars stretching from left eyebrow to cheek. His skin was taunt over a lean structure with barely-there dark facial hair. His eyes were closed as if in sleep, but she knew they were midnight black to match the eyebrows and long straight eyelashes. His face could have been the portrait of a sculpture of a long-ago fighter, or a soldier guardian. Masculinity uncompromised.

She felt a flash of deep overwhelming sadness. She had

teased and taunted this powerful man to get a reaction from him. Just to see if she could gain his attention by getting behind the shield he wielded so effectively. What an immature idiot she had been. Like a kid playing with fire to see how closely she could come to it without getting burned. He had ever right to turn to a woman who met his needs. The bothersome pest that she was held no interest to a mature, courageous man. And that was what Kamon was. An intrepid warrior doing what was required of him. Serving.

Only now with him lying immobile in front of her did she begin to understand the smoldering fire that drove Kamon. The last several months had taught her some important lessons. Willy-nilly behavior, and allowing life to unfold without plan was not how she wanted her life to be. Being spontaneous on a once-in-a-lifetime awanderin' spree was different than having no order to life, where chaos would eventually threaten.

Only now could she understand that the absolute control he exerted over his own body was because of the depth of emotions underneath, not because of a lack of feeling. He felt too much. So much that he had decided that the best way he could function would be to withdrawn from those feelings. To control himself.

Raina turned away to sit quietly beside Kamon, her eyes closed in thought, her emotions saddened as she dealt with the last stage of her grief and loss. Since she had left Shadow Valley she had dealt first with the denial that Kamon was not hers to be. Then anger that he didn't want her as she wanted him. Quickly she had gone through the next stage of bargaining to change herself, then on to depression where she knew she was as she was born to be. This last stage of seeing Kamon ill and helpless brought on the last stage of acceptance. Acceptance that her youthful dreams and ambitions to share Kamon's life forevermore was not to be.

They landed a couple of hours later at Deke's Texas ranch. A station wagon with Deke driving was waiting to move the four of them to the ranch house. After quick hugs and greetings, the men moved the portable gurney with Kamon's limp body to the car, and then drove the short distance to the rambling adobe ranch house.

"I hate your hair," stated Liam flatly, waving a hand toward Raina. "I can understand why you would want to dye it that mouse-brown color, but I still hate it. And it will take years to grow long again. And Sean, you didn't even call or say goodbye, so I think I hate you too!"

"Tough," said Raina with an unconcerned shoulder shrug.

"It's a long story and it all was necessary." Sean soothed, giving Raina a glare. "On my honor. C'mon Liam," coaxed Sean. "Sometimes you have to do stuff. There's no choice."

Liam was silent for a couple of long moments, frowning at Raina and Sean. "I'll accept that. I don't like it though. And I'm still pissed. And if you ever decide to go awanderin' again, at least have the courtesy of letting me know," he groused. "I might not be able to go with you, but I hate being left hanging in the dark."

Brenna waited for them with the door open. "Put Kamon here in the downstairs bedroom," she instructed, leading the way. The twins carefully transferred Kamon to the bed and moved back. A wan-looking Raina watched from the bottom of the bed.

Brenna went through the basic physical motions, mumbling to herself. Deke came in quietly to stand beside Raina. He gave his full attention to Brenna, listening silently to Brenna's examination and her out-loud mutterings.

"You're right, Sean," Brenna announced finally. "He seems to be in a light unconscious state. I can't examine his brain, nor can I take away any of his pain if he has any. To connect with him now would be dangerous to our unborn, and it might be dangerous to me personally. Whatever Kamon experienced was enough to literally disrupt his complete body system. Let's pray that he doesn't …," she stopped as she looked at Raina's ashen face, then at her husband.

Deke moved to Raina, giving her a quick one arm hug. "Hey,

little one. We've all missed you two," His glance included Sean. "A wanderin' does have its own merits though."

"It does," agreed Sean softly. "But it's also nice to be with more family. How do you want to handle shifts to stay with Kamon, Brenna?"

"For now, four hours and I'll take the first one. I just woke up from a nap," she explained.

Raina felt the slight tightening of Deke's hand on her shoulder. "Do you mind if I stay with you? It'll give us a chance for girl talk. And to catch up with all the Shadow Valley gossip."

"Thank you," mouthed Deke silently when Brenna's back was turned.

"I'd like that. You do remember that unconscious persons often hear what's going on around them, so we'll have to keep our girl talk squeaky clean," she stated half in humor.

"Then I guess I'd better see to getting all of you settled. Let me give you a quick tour of the house and your rooms. Then you all can decide what to do," suggested Deke. "Liam, you've got to be tired since you worked all day before you've flown half way across the country and back."

"Nah, you know that flying is fun, not work," grinned Liam. "Oh Sean, you should see the new prototype of the new jumbo jet. Those little green men are going to be so surprised when it's in flight." The three men were laughing together as they exited the room.

"Okay, Raina. You look terrible, not just your hair which I getting used to, but you look ill. What's wrong? Sean said you vomited up your lunch, but that he had eaten the same thing you did and he's fine."

"Truthfully, I feel as bad as I probably look. I just have a massive headache and it's making me sick to my stomach. And I wish to hell people would leave my hair color alone. It's served its purpose extremely well. No one gives me a second glance." She thought a moment than added honestly, "Well a few people did after we removed my facial scar, but not many."

"MAC?" murmured a voice from the bed behind them.

"Kamon. Do you hurt anywhere?" asked Brenna falling back into her primary role as a healer as she hurried toward Kamon's bed.

"No, but I need to tell MAC," he took a deep breath, fighting to stay awake. "Tell MAC that the Mexican punk lied. He lied," his voice slurred, and then stopped as he fell into an exhausted sleep.

"I'll call Catherine and tell her that Kamon needs to tell MAC that whoever it was lied. Sean was right, though. He has exhausted his energy supply, both physically and mentally, to the extent that he is dangerously depleted. He'll need to sleep most of the time for the next several days. Our job will be to make sure he stays hydrated, warm, and takes as much nourishment as he is able."

"Maybe he can tell us what happened then," replied Raina, yawning.

"Why don't you go tell the guys that Kamon woke up for a moment, and maintenance care will be needed. Thankfully, he doesn't seem to be in any pain, just exhausted. Then, Raina, go get a nap. You look almost as bad as Kamon. Which is pretty bad."

"Big sister, I think you're right. I can hardly keep my eyes open. I hate being even a little sick."

Raina found four men in the large great room watching the two-year-old, Brandon, piling colored plastic boxes on top of one another. She barely glanced at the fourth man, merely noting that he was a stranger to her. Guarding her words carefully, she said, "Kamon was conscious for a couple of minutes. Brenna says he's exhausted, and needs rest and maintenance care."

"I'll go see if Brenna needs help now," announced Liam rising to his feet. "See you later, Kurt." He nodded to the fourth man.

"I'll go with you," joined in Sean. "Nice meeting you, Kurt."

"You too," said the cowboy rising to his feet.

"Raina, come in. I want you to meet Kurt Spenser, a friend of mine who also is foreman here at the Circle T. Kurt, this is

Raina Ramsey, Brenna's sister."

"How do you do Raina?" drawled the young cowboy.

"Happy to meet you," said Raina. And she was surprised to realize she was happy to meet him. Kurt wasn't as tall as Deke's six feet four, but he was more muscular through the chest and thighs, probably the result of hard physical labor. His blond hair was cut short and shone in the bright sunlight through the windows. Blue eyes were set in a deeply tanned face, crow's feet attesting to a past of frequent smiles. Kurt wasn't handsome like Eric Shirt, or testosterone-laden like Kamon Youngblood, instead he had the even pleasant features of a healthy all-American male.

Merry blue eyes returned the scrutiny with a grin.

Raina blushed crimson at being caught staring at the man, another new experience for her. Not knowing what to say, she stuttered, "Brenna's ordered me to take a nap. I had some nausea earlier from something I ate."

"Naps are now Brenna's favorite time of day," laughed Deke. "Several naps a day are normal during this pregnancy."

"No. No me nap," insisted Brandon jumping to his feet. "No. No."

Winking at Deke, she gave Brandon a quick hug. "Ahh, come on Brandon, nap with Auntie Raina," she teased.

"No. No. Play Aunt 'Ana. We play," he thrust one of the colored blocks in her hand.

"I'm too tired now, but maybe we can ride horses tomorrow with Daddy. Okay?" she coaxed.

Brandon popped back to his feet. "Horses, horses, Daddy. We ride. Yes, Daddy?"

"You pushed the right button, Raina. This little guy is nuts about horses. He likes horses more than anything else, except maybe cookies."

"Cookies," yelled the little boy.

"My next job since he's finally almost potty trained is to teach him to talk lower than a shout," grinned Deke. "He hasn't quite managed that yet."

Raina had to grin back at Deke. He had come to fatherhood late, and declared that he loved everything about being a dad. His endless supply of patience toward the young toddler was awe-inspiring.

"I take it you ride, Raina. If you ever need someone to ride with you, I volunteer for the job. The ranch is pretty isolated, and it's easy to get lost around here," smiled Kurt. "Mom would definitely be upset if we lost Brenna's sister. She thinks Brenna deserves Sainthood for her volunteer medical work, and for putting up with these two," he waved a hand in Deke and Brandon's direction.

"Kurt's mom is our chief cook and general house boss," explained Deke. "And she spoils this son of ours rotten. More rotten than he normally is," he clarified with a wide grin.

"Well, I don't want to get on any cook's bad side, so nap time for me," yawned Raina. "See you later Kurt."

Both men watched as Raina left the room. When Raina was out of earshot, Kurt asked, "Is Sean Raina's boyfriend or whatever they call it these days? Sean said they were spending the summer sightseeing the Southwest."

"Nope. They are cousins and best friends though, along with Liam. The three of them grew up together and are as close as siblings according to Brenna."

"I've been seeing Megan Bowman for the last five years in an off and on again relationship. Right now we're off and may stay that way. I'm serious and she wants to play some more."

"That's Skip Bowman's younger daughter from the Bar B next door?" asked Deke, striving to maintain neutrality. After a five-year relationship, the off now could be on again tomorrow.

"Yeah, most of us ranch kids grew up together. My brother, Charlie, married Skip's oldest daughter, Suzanne, and they have a little boy, Keith."

"Your mom mentioned that he was the same age as Brandon and she planned on making a play-date for them."

"That sounds like Mom," grinned Kurt." Back to Raina, do you have any objections to my asking Raina to dinner and a movie? I don't want to step over the line if you or Brenna object."

Deke laughed. "I'm sorry, Kurt, but you have to understand Brenna and her sisters," he grinned, eyes twinkling. "They were raised to make up their own minds about anything and everything. No one tells them what they can and cannot do. No one."

He thought for a minute, "Well, they might listen to the oldest sister, but believe me, not to anyone else. So, what you need to do is ask Raina. Personally, I have no objections."

"I'll plan on asking her then. Now back to the original subject, do you want those Angus moved to the south pasture?"

CHAPTER FOURTEEN

Kamon woke slowly, his mind groggy and disoriented. Images floated in the back of his mind like figures on a misty morning. His eyes felt heavy and it was an effort to open them, even into slits. The first thing he saw was Brenna bending over him.

"Back to the living?" she asked quietly.

"Not sure," murmured Kamon keeping his eyes half closed. "I feel like I was in a war that I lost."

"That probably sums it up nicely. Can you tell me what happened? Or at least what you last remember. Just a moment while I get Catherine on a speaker phone, she wants to hear this too."

"Catherine, Kamon's awake. No, its best to just listen and let him tell us as he can. He's still somewhat disoriented. Okay, Kamon, Catherine's listening too."

Taking a slow steadying breath, Kamon's voice was barely audible, "You know about my first visit interviewing Matteus who is an incredibly evil psychopath. And that I was going into international waters to interrogate some potential kidnappers."

He stopped and huffed slowly in and out. "Long story, but this time I was trying to get info from that same psychopath about a possible prison break. An informant said that a South American drug cartel was going to break their leader out of prison, and shoot up a mall. As you know, I had already interviewed," he emphasized the word interviewed, "this guy, Matteus, a couple of weeks before and gained information about some really horrible stuff they had planned in Mexico. MAC stopped that from happening, and cleaned up the mess that it left. I can give you a detailed report later."

Kamon took a deep breath and let it out slowly. "Anyway, going into this guy's mind the second time was different. I had to go into a different part of the brain to see if the raid was planned, and get any details I could, but mostly to check if the informant lied."

"You had to go into the frontal lobe of the brain?" asked Brenna softly.

"Yeah. It was the only way to be sure that plans were made. You know that part of the brain is called the executive function because that's where most of the planning, organizing, changing, etc., takes place. Brenna, I can't tell you of the horror and incredible evil in this man's brain. Like nothing I've ever encountered, even during wartime."

He took another deep breath before continuing, "Pathways were scarred from brutal beatings Matteus had taken as a child. His brain was a living nightmare. There aren't words to tell you how appalling this man's brain was. There were twisted and pitted tissues, matted lumps of scarred damaged flesh. A mass of tangled thought patterns that was vile and criminally insane. Terrifyingly immoral images with little kids involved. Sickening so."

He paused to breath deeply. "Partway though my Mind Walking, Matteus became aware of something wrong between us, and started to yell 'Brujo, Brujo, Witch'. I tried to get out of his mind, and to tell MAC that the informant lied. The last thing I remember was overwhelming nausea, and then being sucked downward toward a black vortex. I knew I was in trouble. I physically tried to move backward but passed out. That's the last thing I remember until I woke up here."

Both Brenna and Catherine were silent, processing what Kamon had gone through.

"Since you have been here I have done nothing except treat you for shock and exhaustion, I'm not sure what you need," Brenna said slowly. "You don't have any physical impairments of any kind that we can find. I found some old injuries that are healed. And I can only examine you physically, externally. I can't connect with you mentally. It could be dangerous for all three of us," she explained holding her hand over her unborn child.

"Don't do anything else," Kamon's voice was forceful. "Brenna, do not bond with me. Under no circumstances. Even if I'm dying. I don't know what that monster did to my mind, or if anything is changed. I could quite literally have part of that demon inside my head."

"Well, we're on the same page then," Catherine interrupted. "Brenna can't bond with you. It would also mean you bonding with her unborn child, and she can't take that chance with the unborn. It breaks my heart to see you in such mental anguish, and know that we can do nothing, Kamon."

"Catherine, Brenna. Right now, I'm just terribly tired like I ran a marathon without water. I don't feel ill. Just exhausted, and disoriented. I'm not sure how much damage has been done to my brain during the time I was connected with Matteus. There's no way for me assess the damage. I can only wait and hope to hell I got out of there in time. If not, we will deal with that too."

"Well, water is plentiful here. It's there on your bed stand. Do you need help?"

"Nope, thanks though." Kamon held the glass in both hands and drank deeply. "How again did I get here? How long have I been here? My brain is fuzzy and unsettled."

Catherine spoke, "I was contacted by a MAC operative and they delivered you to the Monterrey airport, near the California prison where you were. You had shouted that the punk lied. You were unconscious and have remained so until now. Liam took the new drone he was modifying to Lockheed yesterday, so when I called him, he borrowed a plane to pick you up."

"I don't remember any of that," murmured Kamon. "It's all a blank. MAC does know that it was a lie, right? I tried to tell them, but don't know if I succeeded."

"Yes, you did. MAC knows, and they're grateful for your actions. Your companions from MAC said that during your session with the prisoner you slumped over unconscious as he was talking. They said the prisoner went completely berserk, babbling insanely, and fighting the guards. They got you out of there during the chaos. As I said, they called me, and Liam met you in Monterrey then brought you to Brenna in Texas."

"I must have been dreaming. I thought I heard Raina's voice." His voice was barely audible. "I don't know where she is. I have to find her."

Brenna smiled at the anxiety in Kamon's voice. "She's fine. They are having a good trip so far. Learning and doing a lot of things."

"No more. She can't go," Kamon's eyes were closed and his voice began to drift off. "No."

"Brenna," Catherine asked softly. "Is there anything anyone can do? Any backup you need? Anyway, or anyone who can help?"

"Not now," whispered Brenna. "He needs rest now. As for whatever is next. Catherine, I have no way to know what is next. Kamon is too unique, his brain unknown. We have to simply wait, which as you know I'm not good at."

"True," sighed Catherine. "But we don't decide. Not our right, nor is it in our control. So we wait."

When Kamon awoke next, he was more aware of his surroundings, but he had a massive headache. Raina sat beside his bed, staring at him.

"Oh, Kamon, I'm so glad you're awake," she smiled warmly. "We were all so worried. Do you want me to call Brenna? Do you need anything?"

"Your hair, what happened to your hair?" He knew he sounded as groggy as he felt so he fought to keep his voice firm. Her mass of shiny platinum hair had all been cut completely off, leaving only a couple of inches of brown. He blinked in confusion.

Raina run her hands over the short cap of mousy-brown hair. "My hair coloring was too attention-getting so I cut it and dyed it." She dismissed the subject with a shrug of her shoulders as unimportant.

"I don't like it," he complained. "It's ugly."

"Oh good, then we succeeded," she said in a soft, detached

voice. "It's supposed to be nondescript so as to not draw attention. You should have seen me when I had the fake scar on my cheek," she grinned in memory.

Kamon stared back at the woman he had known most of his life as he tried to clear the murkiness from his brain. A woman whom he had sworn to protect with his own life. What was off? What was different? Something was wrong. Drastically wrong. Not only with her hair, but with herself. What had happened to the girl that was Shadow Valley's sunshine, bringing color to his life?

He concentrated trying to get his tired mind to function normally. Usually when she was near him he could feel rays of warmth coming from her, the offshoot of her depth of feelings for him. She exuded caring, of wanting his attention. Her compelling personality and strong will sometimes overwhelmed his mind controls Then she would slip into his personal aura, and he could hear her thoughts even as he tried to block them from his mind.

Now there was nothing. Nothing coming from her. No warmth. No affection or devotion. She gave off the vibrations of a caring acquaintance. Someone he knew, but had little to no relationship with. He swallowed hard trying to come to grips of all that could mean for him.

"We have had a good time," Raina went on unaware of Kamon's confusion. "As ceann-cath you need to know that Sean has been a really good bodyguard and protector. He's been with me all the time. I want to share our adventures with you when you're better, but right now I need to talk to you about something else."

Kamon blinked to hide his turbulent emotions. Only by staying focused could he get through this. This was not the Raina with sunshine hair, crystal blue eyes, and perfect face. This Raina was sending no signals of any kind to his brain, none that he received anyway. No seductive thoughts, no teasing innuendos, no nothing. Nothing. That was it. He no longer had access to her thoughts and feelings. Even non-verbal body ones.

She was closed to him.

He wanted to cuss, and yell. And cry like a baby for his loss.

"Listen Kamon, I only have a few minutes before the others will come in here," Raina insisted, glancing toward the door.

"The others are in here," frowned Brenna striding into the room followed closely by Liam and Sean. "Kamon needs to rest most of all, and to be as stress-free as possible," she scolded without heat. Her frown deepened with the tension in the room. "Now is not the time to look back, or to figure out beginnings and endings. When Kamon is better you can have your private conversations. Until then *my patient*," she paused, "my patient needs to rest his body and his mind. He's been through a harrowing experience that none of us can truly understand. He is not out of the woods yet. Comprende?"

Raina nodded to her older sister in compliance. "Of course. I understand and I'm sorry, Brenna. I should have known better. We can talk later, Kamon."

Before Liam or Sean had a chance to do anything but nod in greeting, Deke walked into the room carrying Brandon on his hip.

"Down, Daddy," Brandon demanded wiggling his little body. "You sick?" he demanded loudly, pointing at Kamon in bed. Glancing at the glare on his mother's face, he put his finger over his lips, "Shhh, mama said."

"Well, that went well. Brandon is now only half-yelling. More like a shout," Liam chuckled. "We wanted to say hello before we went horse back riding. And to see if there's anything you need for us to do."

"Thanks for coming for me and for getting me here," sighed Kamon. "I was out of it. Again, I owe you one Liam. You too Sean. I hear you did a quick med check." Kamon kept his answers short as he grappled with his fatigue.

"Glad I was available. I'm going to stick around until Brenna says I can fly you back to Shadow Valley. Have a mini-vacation," explained Liam. "Catherine has decided that you would be better off there for now."

"Maybe in a week, or less," Brenna answered the question not being asked. "Again, it depends on how fast he heals. For awhile, he's going to rest and do almost nothing." Turning to Sean and Raina, she smiled warmly, "I'm glad the two of you are staying for a few days before resuming your wanderin'."

"Kurt has offered to take us on a short camping trip on horse back. He's rounded up several of his friends from the neighboring ranches to go with us. It should be fun. Oh, and thanks Deke for giving him the time off, we all appreciate it," Sean grinned.

"There's not much going on right now until we have to move some of the horses to the Spring Creek ranch. I'm just sorry that I can't go with you, but I'm on the last chapter of the new book, and want to finish seeing what old Paul Tate is up to. And even more important, I need to be here so that Miss Brenna takes naps regularly."

All of them laughed. Deke wrote a detective series with Tate as lead character. The series was partially based on his own exploits before he met Brenna. No one other than family knew of his secret authorship. And naps seemed to be not only the subject for teasing, but a major part of Brenna's day.

"Daddy, we go," implored Brandon tugging on his Daddy's jeans. "Horses."

"Not this time, Buddy," laughed Brenna. "Remember Keith is coming over to play, and you're going to make cookies with Maude."

A perplexed frown shone on the little boy's face. "No horses?". Looking at his mother's face, he capitulated, "Cookies? Okay," he beamed. Trading cookies for horses was obviously not the little boys first choice, but his mother's word was law.

"Okay Raina? Time to get everything together. Don't forget your boots this time," Sean laughed.

Raina made a face at him, and then smiled happily. "Got it. I'll never live down the fact that I didn't bring my good boots, and ended up buying some at a thrift store in Texas. And they're great boots, so there," she stuck her tongue out at Sean.

"We'll talk soon," Raina smiled broadly, including Kamon and everyone else in the room.

No one questioned Raina's comment. The history of Kamon and Raina was better left unsaid and unquestioned. Kamon's temper was legendary, and Raina's vocabulary could act like a cutting sword. Tangling with either, or both, could bring serious consequences. Stepping between them might be disastrous and sure to accomplish nothing.

Kamon closed his eyes to block out the room of people. He was tired, but irritated, uneasy, and confused as well. Raina was changed. No longer the naïve little girl that demanded his attention. No longer someone he knew. And he felt empty.

"I need to call Catherine. Need to talk with her." His voice began to slur.

"When you wake up again," soothed Brenna. "Just nap for awhile then you can call her." She watched as his body slowly relaxed into sleep. "Okay, everyone out. He needs rest more than anything to heal."

The next time Kamon woke up he fought through the fatigue, knowing that it was imperative that he talk to Catherine. Brenna sat beside his bed, her head back as she dozed.

"Need to call Catherine. Sorry. But important."

Brenna gave a wide yawn. 'That's okay, I drift off to sleep if I even think about sitting down."

"Catherine. Gotta talk to her. And you." Kamon's breath was short and irregular.

"This house isn't set up for anything but good old regular phones. I'll use my cell phone and loud speaker." Dialing a number, she said, "Catherine, Kamon insists he talk to you immediately. As I told you before, I can't find anything wrong with him except exhaustion," she added as she handed the phone to Kamon.

"Catherine? Listen carefully. I don't know how long I can stay awake and aware." There was hitch in Kamon's voice as he continued, "My mind may be damaged now. All I want to do is sleep. And worse, I am concerned that my gift as a Native American Mind Walker may be gone, or at least be impaired."

Brenna didn't bother to hide her gasp of surprise, but Catherine asked in a calm voice, "Why do you think that your mind is damaged? What are your symptoms? What is different?"

"I can do nothing except sleep. And my mind is fuzzy. I can't focus on a conversation much less try to form a thought."

"That's from pushing your body into exhaustion and near collapse," stated Brenna firmly. She placed her hand lightly on his arm. "Catherine, I'm only touching him now and there is an overwhelming tiredness emitting from him everywhere. But I can't feel anything else, especially any deviances or abnormalities."

"Brenna, you know you may not bond with him; however, I am glad to hear that you feel no monsters lurking."

"Now, Kamon as to your gift as a Mind Walker, that will be revealed with time only. Please do not do any Walking until you know what you are missing, or not missing. It would be dangerous for you and perhaps be destructive to other people. Even fatal for both of you. That is an order. Do you both understand?"

"Yes. I think we both understand the seriousness of Kamon's situation. We will both be coming back to Shadow Valley within the week I think" announced Brenna. "I'm unsure about Sean and Raina. They may continue to go awanderin' if you don't have a need for them."

"As to that, I'm unsure about them right now, but see you soon. Kamon, you know how the mind works, your history, as well as our combined one. Remember that please," she said as she hung up.

"Since there's nothing else we can do right now but play out a waiting game, I have another problem," sighed Kamon.

"You're just full of them today, aren't you?" Brenna teased.

Kamon didn't smile. "Raina was here this morning as you know. What you don't know is that I could feel nothing coming from her." Brenna started to speak and was hushed by an upright hand. "Let me finish. I need to say it out loud. Hell, maybe then I will understand it myself."

He took a deep breath and closed his eyes to gather his thoughts. "Raina and I have always had a connection, for want of a better word. I never Walk in her mind, but her inner being is so strong that her feelings come at me in waves. Most of the time my mind-shield works, and she can't enter into my mind. Sometimes it doesn't." He looked directly at the clan healer for help.

Brenna remained silent.

"Today when she was here, I could no longer feel her. There was nothing coming from her to me. Nothing. No warmth, no caring and definitely no passion, again for want of a better word. The mystery is that our inward spirits are no longer connecting in any way. She's no longer available to me. There was a barrier ninety feet high surrounding her."

"In what way?" asked Brenna gently.

"I can't explain it very well. Words do not explain the absence of feelings very well, especially trying to describe what is essentially a void. It's as if sometime since she's been gone awanderin', she's become someone different. Someone I don't know inside and out. Someone whose feeling do not bond, or link with mine. Does that make sense?"

Brenna studied the strong, slim face looking for other signs of distress. She found none.

"It does make sense. Okay, then it seems we have three problems that we must deal with. As your physician I am part of whatever you are, plus whatever happens to you affects the entire clan. Not only are you a cousin and close friend, but you are also the ceann cath of the clan. So we deal with each problem one at a time."

"First, and most important, you're not sure if you removed your Mind Walking from your psychopathic prisoner soon enough. Correct? If you didn't that could make you as insane as he was. Is that right?"

"Harshly said, but true," admitted Kamon. "Matteus was insane. And the kind of evil that you couldn't comprehend. Years of depraved, degenerate, evil behavior."

"Truth only between us. We tell each other the truth, and

how the other person reacts is not up to us. Remember the rule we've always had. The truth," she reminded him referring to the vow Catherine, Brenna, Kamon, and their late cousin, Diane Kaye, had made.

"Yes," murmured Kamon. "I want to know as much as it is possible to do whatever I have to do. Before you ask the obvious, that my gift is somehow my connection to Raina, let me assure you that it isn't. Raina has always been transparent for me. She's honest and direct. I've never walked through her mind as it would be unethical. She's always been linked to me, easy to read and open for me."

"That never entered my mind," smiled Brenna warmly. "You have too much integrity to be sneaky. Besides Raina has always been an open book to most of us. Most of the time what you see is what you get with Raina. And she makes no apologies for that."

"I agree," stated Catherine firmly.

"True, but now she's a closed book, at least to me. And frankly that scares the hell out of me."

"Then let's talk about your three problems one at a time, okay?"

Kamon nodded in agreement.

"If you did not get out in time for Matteus to have given you some of some aberrational thinking, then what can be done? You and I both know that it depends on the extent of the injurious site, where and how much is affected. The only real issue is if you become a danger to others or to yourself. Then of course you will be incarcerated in a place where you can do no harm to yourself or others," she stated matter-of-factly but with a quiver in her voice.

"That would be the choice if it happened to anyone else," Kamon agreed sadly. "What has to be done, will be done. I can never decide if that's because we are Scots, or Native Americans, or just humans trying to survive."

"All probably. Anyway, time is the only way of knowing if, or how much, you have been affected. Or if you have been affected at all. You don't know if you got out of his brain in time or not. Truthfully, no one can know right now. The worst problem for me is that I cannot bond our spirits and minds. It's too dangerous for both of us, plus there's an unborn child to consider."

"No way are you putting yourself or the baby at risk. Under no circumstances could I allow that. I would never be able to survive the consequences if I damaged either of you."

"Agreed. But only time will tell about this first problem, as hard as that is to wait. We will observe you closely to monitor your reactions."

"Now to the second problem. You can't use your gift as a Native American Mind Walker because you don't dare infect another person's brain if you didn't leave Matteus's mind in time. What he gave you, you could give to someone else. If there has been damage to your psyche, and you no longer have the gift the Creator bestowed on you, it does not change who you are."

"The funny part about that is if I'm outside the valley I'm an oddity, even when they don't know the full extent of my gift. During one of the sessions where we were interrogating a wartime prisoner, a special operative called me a freak of nature to a group of other special ops. They all agreed, not knowing that I could hear them. Hell, they just thought that I was highly intuitive, and could read body language. He would have been even more appalled if he had known the truth."

"You know it's a gift, Kamon," Brenna said sternly. "An unasked for Gift. Yeah, dealing with it is sometimes a pain in the butt, but we have little to no choice. I don't remember choosing to look like Grandmother, or to devote my life to healing. And you didn't choose to be who you are. What is, is. Remember?"

"I just hope I still Mind Walk, and can use it for the good."

Ignoring his comment, Brenna continued. "Third is your lack of connection to Raina. It could be several reasons," she stated quietly. "Maybe because of your exhaustion, or Raina is growing up, or a multitude of other things."

Brenna was unwilling to even hint at the what might be the

real reason. Raina might be protecting herself by not allowing any emotional feelings toward Kamon. Something she was not only strong enough to do, but might feel a need to do after seeing Kamon in a potentially intimate setting with someone else. If that was true, Kamon didn't know it yet, but he would have a long road back for Raina to trust him again. And to allow him full access into her emotions. One problem at a time, she reminded herself. I'm a healer, not a magician.

"All I can do now anyway is sleep," Kamon muttered, yawning.

"That I do know how you feel," yawned Brenna in unison.

CHAPTER FIFTEEN

"Is he asleep?" whispered Raina to Sean who was sitting in a chair reading.

"Yes," replied Sean softly.

"I need to talk to him. It's kind of important. At least to me. I probably should wait but I have to do this."

"I'm awake," said Kamon from the bed. "I'm resting my eyes, as Grandfather used to say."

"I remember that," smiled Raina. "That was his magic trick to get us to take a nap when we needed it. I miss him so much that sometimes my entire body hurts."

"Me too," said Kamon and Sean simultaneously.

"Are you up to listening to me for a few minutes, Kamon? It won't take long. I promise."

Kamon was instantly alert. Her voice was a normal tone, not playful or lightly insinuating. No teasing. No engaging behavior and no warmth. No wanting to be a part of him. As if she was talking to Mrs. Searle or to Fergus. She was standing beside the bed, her beautiful face solemn in its seriousness.

And she hadn't touched him.

Ever since she had hit puberty she had touched him at every opportunity, on his shoulder, or just letting her fingers glide down his arm. He had always said that it irritated him, but now he missed the fiery, shivery feel as her fingers glided lightly over his skin. Now her hands were folded neatly in front of her, nowhere near his own body.

Sean started to get up out of the seat to leave, but Raina put up a hand to stop him. "Please stay, Sean. As my bodyguard we have no secrets, remember?" Turning back to Kamon, she sighed, "And in truth, I want to say it aloud now."

She took a deep breath and blew it out slowly. "I want to

apologize for all the times I've teased and taunted you. I'm sorry for trying to get a reaction from you, any reaction. Like a child, a negative response was almost as good as a positive one. You paid attention to me for a moment which is what I wanted." She chewed her bottom lip for a moment, before going on, "I flirted outrageously with you, and you had no choice but to be as nice as you could be, which was mostly to ignore me. My crush lasted for a long time, and I put you through a difficult time I'm sure."

Kamon leaned forward, sitting up in the bed. "Raina...," he began.

"No. Please don't attempt to justify my actions as a young girl trying out her wiles on an older, safe man. That's not true, but nevertheless I was wrong. I didn't have a right to put you into a situation that took away your choices. And the choice was yours. I'm sorry, and I will not behave that way again. I hope you can find it in your heart to forgive me," Raina said as she blinked back tears.

"Of course," replied a stunned Kamon, unsure how to react.

"Thank you," Raina said softly as she turned and fled the room.

Kamon glanced at Sean who remained stone-faced and unsmiling. "I'm shocked and astonished. I didn't expect anything like that reaction, ever. That was a different Raina than I've seen before."

"Yeah," Sean commented noncommittedly.

"Did something happen on your trip? Did she meet someone? Is that why?"

"I'm sorry Kamon, but you'll have to ask Raina that. I wouldn't feel right in guessing her motives. I will say that we do all grow up. Raina is Raina," he shrugged his shoulders in acceptance.

Kamon lay back and closed his eyes. His life was going to hell in a hand basket. First the disaster with Matteus, and now Raina. Four months ago, he was a happy man thinking that life was good, and now his entire future was an uncertain quagmire. He could mentally gear himself up to wait to see if exhaustion was the primary reason for his present mental state. His mind would either be deranged or not.

But Raina? She had always been in his peripheral vision since her teen years. She wasn't for him, but he had always felt better knowing where she was, and if she was safe. This Raina was no longer the bouncing, flirty young woman who teased him mercilessly. She had always been self confident, but with this new maturity she was also self-contained and detached. An individual he didn't know. Now he was no longer a part of anything she did. Sean was her bodyguard, and her friend. He had no role to play. How could he accept that she wouldn't be in his life now? That her future would be one without him? Completely without him in it.

For Kamon the next few days were anticlimactic. Nothing happened. He felt a little better physically after a few days of sleeping around the clock, but there didn't seem to be any changes to his mind, at least that he could tell. He didn't feel any different than before his interrogation of Matteus, but since the entire experience was new, he couldn't decide if that was a good thing or not. He tried to examine his own mind, but it was a useless proposition. How could he tell what was different and what was not? Him versus Him.

Raina dutifully visited him every day to ask how he was feeling. She was always with someone else, never lingered, or indicated that she was interested in spending more time with him. She was smiling and polite, treating him as if he was an older distant cousin. Which he was.

And it was eating him up alive.

Five days later Brenna declared Kamon fit to travel. She had not found any signs that his condition was getting worse, although he was only marginally better. After a consultation with Catherine, they had decided that the best place for him was in the seclusion of Shadow Valley, but staying in his old apartment at the Stone House instead of returning to his own home. She and Brandon would also travel with Liam as well as Sean and Raina who had decided to return to the valley, at least temporarily.

Kamon leaned back in the airplane seat with his eyes closed. The last couple of days had been hellish. Nothing in his past could have prepared him for the devastation he felt. There were still no symptoms of erratic behavior nor hallucinations. No bouts of agitated activity akin to Matteus. It was like waiting for a bomb to drop, praying that you would be missed, having no control and unsure of the outcome. Those problems made his head hurt.

And the problem with Raina made his heart ache. He had mulled over all the differences between them, their ages and experiences mainly. Their opposite personalities, hers sunny and his dour. He could make her unhappy. She could make him Superman. He felt incomplete now without the connection between them. It would not be fair to pursue a relationship with her. He wanted her. He wasn't for her. She was grown up. He was part of her past. Going round and round in his mind in a never-ending circle. He felt adrift as if he was floating with no direction, no sense of purpose. And the pain and uncertainty were ever present.

Waiting had to be the worst punishment created for mankind. It left the heart heavy, and the mind in a tangled web of thoughts. And feeling vulnerable and powerless.
He hated not being in control of his facilities and thereby his life. And he was just so damn tired of being tired that his thinking wasn't clear.

What he did know that he had to somehow reconcile his relationship with Raina. If the sickness was in his mind, he had to bow completely out of her life as gracefully as possible.

Raina was startled by the ringtone of her phone as she dozed in one of the recliners on the plane. Only Catherine used that special sound. Raina had been in that place between sleep and awake, the land of lite dreaming. Now reality came crashing in. Catherine never called just to chat, her world was too busy and responsibilities too great.

"Catherine?" Raina asked.

"There's a problem here and I wanted to alert you to what we need before you land. A young woman showed up at the gates this morning. She was driving an older beat up car. She claims that her grandmother told her to come here to Shadow Valley if something happened to her grandmother, but she says she doesn't know why."

Raina could hear Catherine's deep indrawn breath, then the equally deep exhale. "Normally this would be a security problem and would be Kamon's jurisdiction, but there's no way he can handle this now. I need you to interview her instead. I can't ask Brenna, or anyone else. You are sensitive to nuances and can feel when a person is telling the truth or not. Frankly, Raina, I don't know what is truth about her and what is not, and I have my hands full here. According to Alma, she seems sincere but …. You know there's a huge risk if outsiders …," again she paused.

Raina interrupted. "The most important thing for you is taking care of that baby that is due next month, Catherine. Brenna said you might have to go on bed rest again if there's a problem. I know you hate that." Raina reminded her lightly.

Raina continued, speaking softly, "I will go over to talk with her immediately. Where is she now? Who has seen her, or worse yet who has she seen?" Raina kept her tone mater-of-fact. No use getting excited about something until she had more information. She grinned in spite of the seriousness of the problem. She was sounding more like her brother-in-law Trent every day, wanting more information.

"Mr. MacPherson is in Scotland on an errand for me, but Alma is there. I explained the situation and Alma said she would be glad to help. She drove down to the gate and the young woman followed her home. Their place is out of the way of other houses if you use the back way, and Alma understands the significance of this. And how serious it could get."

"Then she hasn't had any contact with anyone except Alma?"

"Not as far as we know. She told Alma that her grandmother had given her directions to the valley, and told her not to stop anywhere until she got there. According to what she told Alma she followed exactly what she said her grandmother told her to do. She didn't stop anywhere except for gas, and she did not stop in Spring Creek."

"Thanks Catherine, I'll do the very best I can without Kamon. Sean and I will head over there as soon as we land. I will let you know if I can find what her truths are, or are not. Then you can decide what the next step should be."

"You can tell Sean, Liam and Brenna. I would prefer that you don't involve Kamon until after I talk to Brenna and to Kamon face to face. I need to see him myself to decide."

"Okay, but you know he's going to be pissed later. He takes his duties very seriously. And he may feel that I'm stepping into his territory, which I am." Raina would follow Catherine's dictates and deal with the aftermath later. Kamon's ire included.

"Then I'll talk with you as soon as you know something. You and Sean might want to change into your oldest clothes. No telling what you will be facing. And maybe put together a back story."

"Good idea. Catherine, are you really okay?" Raina stressed the word you.

"Yeah, I'm fine. This baby is more active than Alexa was. I'm positive he has 4 feet and 6 sharp elbows. Oh, and his favorite sport is football. And he's joining the Cavaliers as soon as he gets out of his womb prison."

"It's a boy? Cavaliers? I didn't know that it was a boy, but Catherine I think the Cavaliers are a basketball team."

"Then maybe the Whatever's. We don't know the baby's gender, but Trent and Maggie both insist the baby is a he, so Alexa, Doug and I are going along with them. I've got to go now, but Raina I'm really glad you're coming home for a lot of reasons. Love you."

Raina smiled as she looked at the dead phone she still held. No goodbyes. Catherine was Catherine. And Kamon was going to be more than pissed when he found out he had been taken out of the protection loop.

She stopped just inside the airplane doorway separating the seating area from what had now become Brenna's clinic area. Kamon was laying on his side facing her with his eyes closed in sleep. At least Raina hoped it was in sleep. He had spent the last four days in and out of sleeping sessions. Brennan had said that his body had simply shut down from the trauma of his last two months, especially Mind Walking through Matteus's madness.

She leaned to the side to gain a different view. He looked the same as he did before she left, maybe a little leaner in the face. The two thin scars running down from his left eyebrow to his cheek was a little more pronounced. He needed a haircut or at least a trim. His black hair had become partially loose from the throng holding the mass of hair at the nape of his neck. She started forward to put her hand on his forehead to check for heat, then stopped.

She would no longer take the initiative when Kamon was involved. No matter how she felt, he was not hers, and could never be. He still made her heart race even though one part of her felt unjustifiable betrayal. She had apologized for her own actions, but her heart wanted what it wanted. Grandfather Youngblood said that time heals. Healing couldn't come soon enough as far as she was concerned. And she wished the hell it would hurry up.

She realized that she had been standing staring at Kamon for several minutes. Brenna stood beside the medical gurney watching her with a questioning look on her face. Raina motioned for her to come nearer, and quietly relayed Catherine's message. Brenna simply nodded her understanding. Raina knew that Brenna seldom questioned her older sister. Their spheres of knowledge gave them a different perspective, and each respected that in the other. Their areas of influence were in completely different areas of service.

Raina went forward to the cockpit where the twins were talking quietly so as not disturb Kamon's sleep. She relayed Catherine's message to them, then asked Sean to go with her to the MacPherson's to talk with the young woman as Catherine had asked.

"Raina, have you forgotten that I go where you go if its outside the normal?" Sean grinned. "That's what bodyguard means," he chided. "It means I guard your body where that body is."

"It's the hair dye," teased Liam. "It's soaked into her brain and caused early dementia."

"You too are idiots just like I always said," laughed Raina rolling her eyes dramatically as she left the front of the plane.

Why couldn't her heart want Sean or Liam? Or Eric Shirt, or anyone else she had met. Somehow, she was that oddity that had fallen in love at thirteen years old and so far had stayed that way. Of course it hadn't helped that Kamon was built like a warrior of old with muscular chest, long legs, and striking features. And his skin made her hands itch. Warm, bronze and sexy.

Shaking her head to dislodge her thoughts, she focused on the little she knew about the upcoming meeting with the young woman who had invaded the valley. As far as she knew, no one had entered Shadow Valley without permission in her lifetime. Intriguing and scary.

And now that Kamon was incapacitated, it was her responsibility to separate truth from fiction. She took a deep breath, and closed her eyes. And prayed that she would be up to the task before her.

CHAPTER SIXTEEN

The landing at Sanhicks airport in Shadow Valley went smoothly as did Kamon's transfer into a modified station wagon. During the flight, Kamon seemed to fall into a deeper sleep, but woke at intervals seemingly in no pain. Brenna seemed a little concerned about Kamon's increasing need to sleep, but little could be done until he could be examined again at the Stone House.

The added benefit of moving him into the bustling residence was that it would guarantee that he wasn't isolated, but could be if that was required. And Brenna could monitor her very pregnant sister as Catherine progressed toward the end of her last trimester. And she could nap, although that was less an issue now in her own beginning second trimester of pregnancy.

Raina had decided that since they couldn't help with Kamon, that she and Sean would go from the airport directly to the MacPherson's to check on the outsider. She had kept the dyed shaggy haircut, and now applied some of the shallow facial makeup. She and Sean both wore the low-cost jeans and shirts from the thrift store that had served them so well in their travels. Now well worn and a tad frayed, the clothes had become their manual labor uniforms.

Sean pulled his dark green pickup to the front of the large semi-Victorian home where the MacPherson's lived. Wide wooden porches wrapped around three sides of the huge one-story older home. White wicker couches, chairs and table were interspersed with a plethora of green plants. Alma MacPherson was famous for her green thumb; a broken shrub branch became another vibrant plant under Alma's care.

Alma opened the door before they knocked. "Good thing

Catherine warned me about your hair, Raina, it's quite a shock. And you're Anna and Shane. Mary is lying down in Susan's old room," she whispered referring to her daughter. "She's only told me a little about herself, she seems to be expecting something or someone else. I like her. But there's something …," she left the rest unsaid as they entered the great room.

The MacPherson's home was Raina's second favorite private home in the valley. Her absolute favorite was the cedar and glass home Kamon had built. The MacPherson's home was built of wood a generation before, but had been completely remodeled for the MacPherson's and their four children. Now those children were grown or away at schools. The open great room had a huge fireplace, wooden floors and comfortable yet elegant furniture.

"I thought I head someone talking," a young woman said softly, stepping into the room from the hallway. About five four, brown hair cut to shoulder length, a slender body and an oval face. Her face was neither plain nor beautiful, she would have been deemed average by most. Except for her eyes. Her eyes were a hazel green mixture with thick dark lashes and brows to match.

"Hello, I'm Anna and this is Shane," Raina said, dropping back into the names they had used awanderin'. "We're part of the security team for the wildlife sanctuary." A half truth. Sean smiled, nodded, but didn't speak. They had decided that Raina would keep the focus on herself until she needed him to step into the conversation. His duty as her bodyguard.

"How do you do? I'm Mary Garcia."

Raina kept her composure, but she was surprised to hear a Latin last name.

"Please sit with us," Alma requested as she indicated the place beside Raina on the sofa.

Raina sat quietly, hands folded in her lap as she watched Mary Garcia take a seat beside her. As long as she was within the person's personal aura with no barriers between them, she could open herself to focus on feelings that were emitted.

Even after Mary sat down beside Raina on the sofa, she

looked across at Alma for guidance. She did not look at Sean at all.

She's scared to death Raina realized. Her fear is emitting from her in waves. What the hell? Why the intense fear? For being caught in a lie? From something else that had nothing to do with us? What?

"Mary, why don't you tell us a little about yourself," smiled Alma warmly. "Tell me again how you found the valley?"

"My grandmother told me that if anything ever happened to her that I needed to come here." She didn't elaborate.

"Did she tell you why?" asked Alma gently.

Mary nodded her head no.

"Where did you come from?" asked Alma.

"A little town near Albuquerque, New Mexico."

Raina spoke for the first time since introductions. "Alma said you needed some help. We need to know who you are for us to do that. It's difficult to help you if we know nothing about you." She kept her voice soft, but her tone was neutral.

Mary bowed her head, letting her long hair cover most of her face. "I lived in Albuquerque, I grew up there," and again lapsed into silence.

"Mary, you need to tell us more about yourself, and how we can help you. With one sentence answers, it will take us a week from next Sunday to help."

Mary remained silent with her head down.

Well its bluff time, Raina thought standing up. "Alma, would you please show Mary how to get out of the valley. This is private property, a wildlife sanctuary. Be sure she has enough gas to get to Spring Creek."

Mary gasped. "You're kicking me out? I can't just stay here? Can you do that?"

"Yes, I actually can do that. This is private property."

Raina continued, "I will only say this once. Alma thinks you may need some help so I'm   withholding judgment, but I hate being played. If you want help, I will be happy to listen."

"Please, sit down," Mary's eyes glistened with tears. "I just don't know whom to trust. Grandmother said to come here, and I would be safe in the mountains. And she mentioned a Maeve Ramsey."

Her grandmother, Maeve Ramsey, had been dead for several years. She had traveled extensively, so anyone could have accessed her name. "How did your grandmother know Maeve Ramsey?"

"I don't know. She never mentioned her until the last week, just before she died."

Raina sat back down, but Sean leaned against the fireplace mantle, his body language telling Raina he was skeptical of this young woman. Maeve Ramsey had been dead for more than five years; why would she tell her granddaughter last week? It made little to no sense at all.

"If you want us to help you, you have to give us more information. Maybe you need to start with when you were born, and tell us your life story. And Mary, we can't help you if you tell us a pack of lies."

Mary looked from Alma then back at Raina.

"Do you want to talk now, Mary, because frankly I'm tired, cranky, and frustrated? I've just came home from a long trip, and I want to go home myself." Cards on the table time, thought Raina irreverently, just like Kamon would have done. She leaned back against the sofa, feigning tiredness. With her eyes at half-mast, it was easier to connect with her feelings.

Mary's words began hesitantly. "I don't know where I was born, there is no birth certificate. I only have vague memories of living with my parents in a cabin in the mountains of Montana. It was the three of us and I don't remember any neighbors. My mother's name was Erica, she was pretty and kind. I remember sitting on her lap while she brushed my hair. All I remember about the man was that he yelled and beat my mother. And I had to hid. One night the police came and took my mother and me away. They told me she went to the hospital and I never saw her again. My grandmother came and got me. I had never seen her before. We went to New Mexico and lived in San Semas, a little town outside Bernaillo, New Mexico. It's near Albuquerque." She paused in thought.

Mary lifted her head, but kept her eyes cast downward, not meeting anyone's eyes. "My grandmother's name was Juanita Gonzales. She was the most wonderful person you could have imagined. She was smart, warm-hearted and gave the best hugs ever." A single tear drifted unnoticed down her left cheek. "And stubborn. Angie said that grandmother could out-stubborn Oscar the mule. Angie Apodaca was grandmother's friend and boss. Angie's family owned the trading post on the Sandia Reservation where grandmother worked as a book-keeper."

The cadence of the spoken language washed over Raina as she allowed Mary's feelings to take shape in her mind. She let her mind accept and examine each word to see if the essence of the spoken word matched the word's reality. Truth and fiction.

"Did you go to school in Albuquerque?" asked Raina softly, needing to check the answer but also trying to keep Mary rambling.

"No. Grandmother took me with her to the Sandia Pueblo. I went to the elementary school there, but the rest of my education was from on-line schools." Mary waited to see if Raina would ask something else.

Raina remained silent.

Finally, Mary fidgeted and said "Grandmother got breast cancer two years ago. She had treatments but it was too late. She died four days ago. She had bought Angie's grandfather's old car and told me to use it to come here."

Sean's phone rang before she could say anything else. "Yeah. Okay. Be right there." Turning to Raina, he said "Sorry, we need to leave." He gave no explanation why.

Raina turned to Alma. "We'll be back as soon as we can," Raina said including both Alma and Mary.

"Go, go child. Mary can stay with me for awhile. There's no problem."

Raina knew that the warm, affectionate woman was also very, very smart. She had been part of Shadow Valley most of her life and understood the significance of outsiders. Vows would never be broken by Alma MacPherson.

Raina remained silent until they got into Sean's truck. "What?" she demanded, her voice breaking. "Catherine? The baby?"

"Kamon. He's developed a high fever and is asking for you."

Raina felt like she had been hit hard in the stomach. Tears glistened but she swallowed hard. Nothing could happen to him. He was too vital. Too alive. And no matter how he felt, she was still connected to him.

"Mary. Telling the truth or not?" asked Sean trying to divert Raina's thoughts even if only for a moment.

"Both. Some of it true, but most wasn't. Her grandmother's name, her name, and much of her past was a lie. She's omitted most of the important things in her life. She's not naive or innocent. Oh, and she's playing a younger self than she really is. I hate being played. Right now, she's just a total bother."

Raina rubbed her hands hard over her face her mind returning to Kamon. What could possibly have happened? He had no fever when they had left the airplane, although he had been sleeping very soundly. Or had Brenna chose not to tell her? Damn. She would have never gone to check out Mary if she had known that Kamon was seriously ill. Even though there was nothing she could have done, her spirit needed to know where he was. And that he was safe.

CHAPTER SEVENTEEN

Raina stood beside the hospital bed normally used for clinic patients that had been moved to Kamon's room. Brenna stood on the other side, her stethoscope on Kamon's chest. His breathing was harsh and his face was ashen. Sean and Liam stood at the back of the room awaiting any orders from Brenna.

Brenna motioned Raina to step outside the room with her, closing the door gently behind them.

"What happened?" asked Raina softly. She knew that even when Kamon was unconscious he could still hear, and maybe process whatever they were saying. A mistake that many people made in hospitals, not realizing that an unconscious person was aware at some level.

"Kamon is in and out of consciousness," Brenna spoke in a low voice. "His fever is high, fluctuating between 102 and 104. He keeps mumbling your name, Raina." She gave a huge sigh. "The biggest problem for me is that I can't connect with him, it's too dangerous for the baby and for me. The first thing I have to rule out is if it is connected in some way with his Mind Walking with Matteus." She straightened her spine to stretch her back muscles. "I don't think it is, but I have to be sure."

"If it's something not related to his episode with Matteus, then it looks like a viral infection of some kind. I've taken blood and sent Tommy to take it down to Fortuna to be tested. For now, my tentative diagnosis is that he has contracted the Kunjin virus. It's spread by mosquito bites and he could have gotten it in Mexico when he went to rescue those girls. It's a close relative to the West Nile virus."

"Brenna, I'm totally in the dark about where he was, or

why. Bottom line, Brenna, how serious? Talk to me Brenna," said Raina impatiently.

"I'm going to sound like all doctors but it depends on what happens next. We're trying to rule out any connection with Matteus. It has been a little more than a week and there no sign of any deviances. And I've observed almost hourly. But the truth is I don't know for sure."

She continued. "Now if this is the Kunjin virus, about one percent of people who are infected develop severe neurological illnesses like encephalitis or meningitis. You know that's inflammation of the brain and surrounding tissues."

"And that's not whole truth, is it? I feel you are withholding information from me. What else, Brenna? What are you not telling me?" Raina's voice was rising in agitation.

Brenna grimaced in concentration. "I'm try to separate his Mind Walking from a viral infection, each of which may have affected Kamon's brain. Simply put, what is from his Mind-Walking episode with Matteus, and what is the possibility he was bitten by mosquitos in Mexico?" She held up in hand in the time-honored gesture of stop. "The difference is that if it's from a primary source that is directly from a mosquito, then the illness may be milder."

"And the prognosis, either way? He will get well, right?" Raina swallowed hard fighting down the nausea which threatened.

"The problem with Matteus is on hold, there's no way to know for sure yet although I feel that Kamon is not affected. The other factor is that most people recover from Kunjin fever. The bad news is that if he develops other symptoms or it's a severe case of Kunjin fever, there is no absolute cure."

She hugged Raina tightly. "He mumbles your name over and over in his delirium. Now is the time in your life where your training is needed. More stress on Kamon will seriously replete his energy levels, and he needs every ounce of energy to fight whatever this is. You two have a deep connection whether its future or past."

Brenna stepped back and looked directly into the crystal-blue eyes of her younger sister. "You are Raina Ramsey, with responsibilities and knowledge. What Kamon needs now is your support, not mine, and not even Catherine's. Yours. For whatever reason, he needs you now."

Raina stood taller. "And that's what he will get always, Brenna. You're right. We have a deep relationship. Somehow we've always had a special connection, even when he thought I was just a pest. And I'll stay here until you tell me he no longer needs me."

"I was hoping you would volunteer before I asked you. What about the young woman at Alma's?"

"She's telling some truths, and some lies. Sorting it out may take some time. Time that I don't have right now, and quite frankly don't even want to think about. Alma is willing to let her be a house guest for a few days. I'm going to ask Liam and Sean to check some computer sites to verify some other things that I didn't ask."

"In other words, you do have it covered, little general," teased Brenna with admiration in her voice.

"For now. As for the future, as the Creator wills." Raina gave back the words so familiar to the Ramsey sisters.

Kamon eyes opened slowly, unsure of his surroundings. His left hand was warm. He peeped through his eyelashes to survey where the enemies were. The young woman sitting beside him was familiar, but his mind was too foggy to make a connection. Was she a part of the war? An enemy? Should he take her out? Or wait? Where were the other translators? And where was the sand that blew constantly making it difficult to breath, or eat, or move?

"Kamon?" the young woman asked in a soft voice.

He didn't answer. "Don't give them any information about yourself", was the first mantra of field black ops. One slip and a lot of comrades could be dead. Better he died than a bunch of others who had people back home that cared for them. He had no one. Grandfather Youngblood that's all. He couldn't count cousins, not even his best friends, Catherine and Brenna Ramsey. Their little sister, Raina. Not a friend, and could never be anything. Young. So young. Innocent. He felt a sharp prick in his right arm. A shot. Please, don't let it be sodium pentothal. Please. Can't give away secrets. He drifted back into a drug-induced sleep. A couple of hours later, he aroused enough to take a small drink of water, but returned to his horrendous nightmares almost immediately without ever fully awakening.

Raina wept silently as she listened to Kamon's mumblings as he relived the horror of war. He was back in some war-torn country, and thought he had been captured. His fever gave him hallucinations, and his temperature had risen to dangerous levels. He uttered words in Syrian and then in Lebanese, sometimes incoherent sounds. At other times, he blurted out sentences which sent chills through her as he talked about blood and deaths.

His anguish increased as he relived what the war-ravaged countries had done to children, and to the families. A place with no schools, little food, and what had become the normalcy of seeing early deaths. Kids who didn't know anything except to live in a war-torn country. Living in rubble for homes with no heat and little water. And the ever present, over-riding destruction.

For the first time she learned of his hospitalization for broken bones, and the ensuing infections from an explosion. And his need to come home to Shadow Valley where his soul could regroup and heal. He rambled on and on and on, eventually falling asleep from exhaustion only to awaken to more horrific nightmares. Finally, after hours of utterances, he fell into another deep sleep.

Sean, Liam, and Brenna all tried to relieve her from her bedside vigil, but Kamon became agitated and physically restless when she wasn't there. Even with his eyes closed in restless sleep, he seemed to be aware of her presence in the room. As long as Raina remained in the room with him he was calmer, his confusion less overt. Brenna went in and out checking Kamon, but it was only when Raina was near that he became less agitated.

Brenna had talked Kamon's unexpected illness over with Catherine, and had called a Neurologist friend working for the Mayo Clinic for a consultation. She hadn't told him all the story, but had indicated that her patient had been to Mexico. They discussed the research which indicated that mosquitos infected with the Kunjin virus disease had been found in the area where Kamon had been. Her consult told her what she already knew but needed verifying, it was Kunjin fever. The diagnosis was correct, the prognosis uncertain, and it was a waiting game.

When Kamon woke up Brenna would share the good news with Kamon. The cause of the fever was from a virus, and not from his Mind Walking contact with Matteus. The results of that contact with Matteus was still uncertain, but less worrying as time passed.

Raina had chosen to sleep on a chaise lounge in Kamon's room, dragging the heavy recliner parallel to his bed within easy reach of her hand. She awoke on the morning of the third day as Sean tapped her on the shoulder, and mimed the gesture for eating as he held out a covered tray.

She shook her head no. She pointed to the bathroom instead, and indicated without words that Sean needed to watch over Kamon while she used the bathroom. When she returned, Brenna was in the room also.

"You either eat something, or I'm going to ban you from this room and I do mean that, Raina. You've eaten very little since you've been here. You can't help if you don't have the energy. Enough. Mrs. Searle's has made you an egg and cheese omelet. It's light and shouldn't upset your stomach. And it needs to be eaten now. Do you understand?" Brenna raised an eyebrow in question, her voice firm and serious.

Raina took the tray back from Sean. Brenna never bluffed. She meant exactly what she said. She would eat or Brenna would ban her from Kamon's room.

"Raina?" Kamon's voice was raspy and hoarse sounding. "Eat."

"Kamon, you're awake," breathed Raina, fighting back tears.

"Eat," came the hoarse response.

"Welcome back my friend," Brenna said softly. "I won't be stupid enough to ask how you feel."

"Does the word like crap mean anything to you? I will talk to you after Raina eats."

Raina immediately picked up the tray and started shoveling the omelet into her mouth, her eyes never leaving Kamon's face. Both Brenna and Sean laughed.

"Has she eaten it all?" questioned Kamon, his eyes still closed.

"Yes, she has," answered Brenna with a laugh. "More like gobbled it down. Now what can you tell me?"

"Well, my head is pounding, my joints ache, and I couldn't fight off a baby kitten." He stretched his back, "Oh and all my muscles hurt. I've had better days," he blew out a breath. "And I badly need to use the bathroom if you girls will excuse me." He swung his feet to the side of the bed and started to rise. He would have fallen flat on his face if Sean hadn't caught him.

"Okay, I'll help." At Kamon's frown, Sean added "Just this once, until you get on your feet."

Brenna and Raina left the room barely containing their giggles. Neither could have said if their mirth was because of Kamon's macho attitude, or the sheer joy of him being better.

Sean stuck his head out a few minutes later and waved them back in.

Brenna immediately returned to Kamon's side, taking her stethoscope out to check his vital signs. She told him briefly that he had contracted Kunjin fever, a viral infection passed from a bird to a mosquito. "It is now one of the many diseases that mosquitos have contacted who breed in the wetlands. Mexico has a notoriously bad drainage system in many places."

"The girl's families lived in the barrios, the worst of the worst. They are unharmed and will get help. Damn, I'm tired."

"Close your eyes then, nap for a little while. You are going

142

nowhere today except to the bathroom and then only with help."

"There's no way I'm staying in this damn bed," Kamon declared forcefully.

"That damn bed is your damn bed and you will stay there today. And that's a damn order."

Raina burst our laughing. "Kamon, you're an idiot. An absolute imbecile if you think you can intimidate Brenna. She gives the orders," she giggled, "she does not take them."

Everyone turned to look at Raina. Their faces reflected emotions from shock to amusement. No one had ever called out Kamon, or laughed at him. Not ever.

Raina shrugged her shoulders unconcernedly as she noted their reactions. "Well, he is being an idiot. Brenna has become more and more like Grandmother the older she gets. And I love that. Besides she's pregnant which makes her snarky and cranky to begin with," she smiled broadly taking the sting out of her words.

Kamon stared at Raina. She had never treated him with less than adoration, and deference. Or had ignored him as she had done at Brenna and Deke's ranch in Texas. Before, she had thought he was perfect even when his behavior bordered on insulting. And she had just called him an idiot and an imbecile. The girl he had known was no longer. In her place was a young woman who was at least his equal. And now his problems with Raina had only increased, not diminished.

Stifling a yawn, he asked Brenna, "If I'm really well-behaved, may I sit in a chair? I'll be ever so good," he promised in self mockery.

"Not today, tomorrow we'll see. I will need to give you another blood test in two weeks to see if there is a change in the antibody levels. Mostly you're physically in good shape, but you are going to be extra tired for a couple of weeks."

Kamon yawned, trying to stay alert. "I hate this."

"Sean, would you please stay this morning? When he wakes up, he can have a shower but he may need a little help. If he doesn't return to the bed, call me."

"I'm suppose to tattle on you, Kamon? Well that will be a change," Sean grinned at the older man. "You do know that Liam and I were in total awe of you our whole lives. Let's see, follow Kamon's orders, or Brenna's orders?" He looked from one to the other smiling. "Brenna, I'm yours. I do believe right now you could take Kamon. I'll tell you if he's out to self-destruct, we need him too much."

Kamon didn't have enough energy to retort that it seemed that Sean too had changed since he had gone awanderin'

CHAPTER EIGHTEEN

"**K**amon's had a tough week," Catherine said as she and her two sisters lounged in Catherine's sitting room off her office. "Catch me up, Brenna, and then we can talk about our stranger, Raina."

"I'm glad that you, Alexa, and Trent have moved back to the Stone House temporarily. It makes it easier to monitor your pregnancy, and oversee Kamon's problems at the same time," commented Brenna idly.

"We love our house and the privacy it gives us, but my work is here," answered Catherine. "I'm only working a few hours a day, and Trent's in charge of Alexa with the help of everyone in the Stone House. He spoils her rotten, but that's a whole other issue. And we both miss Maggie and Douglas so much. When they decided to go to school this year in Scotland, I thought Trent was going to cry."

She gave a little sniff. "Trent said that Douglas had came to him to tell him that he would watch out for Maggie, and that he would probably have to marry her someday because she was a handful."

"Those two are the most awesome kids," smiled Brenna. "And he's so used to taking care of her, he just might."

Maggie and Douglas were gifted orphans born on the same day from different parents in different parts of the world. Trent and Catherine were their guardian parents.

"To another subject," Catherine smiled. "I've put off or delegated most of the work. Hey, I even found out that the word delegate wasn't a four-letter word," she laughed, her facing lighting up with happiness. "Now, let's talk about Kamon."

Raina looked back and forth between them, but remained silent. Her sister's roles and responsibilities were paramount to the successful running of Shadow Valley.

"Raina needs to know about Kamon's injuries. They may all need to know the possibilities. Everything. The safety of the tribal clan is all our jobs. Decisions will have to be made if things don't turn out like we pray they will."

"Okay, your call," answered Brenna. Gazing at Raina with sadness on her face she said, "Long story short. Kamon was helping MAC with a prisoner, and may have been caught inside the mind of a madman. We don't know the extent of the damage, or even if there is any damage to his mind. I don't dare connect with him on a deep level, it might harm me and my unborn. Our ancestor's dictates are clear on that."

"Then it isn't just exhaustion with this Kunjin virus?"

"Those played a role in his physical disabilities, but the major problem is that his mind may be affected. And we don't know."

"What a nightmare for him," Raina whispered. "Not only picking up some weird mosquito infection somewhere, but having to worry about the possibility of becoming something he isn't. Couldn't be."

Brenna glanced at Catherine, gaining permission. At Catherine's assertive nod, she continued. "Unfortunately, that may not be all of it. If," she emphasized the if, "If he does not have brain damage from the prisoner's insanity, he may no longer have the gift of Mind Walking."

Both sisters watched quietly as their youngest sister assimilated this new information.

Raina sat silently for several minutes, considering all the aspects of what made up Kamon Youngblood. She closed her eyes to create more focus and to dig deeper into her own psyche. Finally, she opened her eyes to look at her sisters, wiping away the tears from her cheeks.

"Kamon is so much more than a Mind Walker. He's a warrior, a fighter. He's a strategist, and would die for the ideals he believes in. He was delirious much of the time during the first few days that I stayed with him."

"He was less agitated when you were in the room," reminded Brenna.

"I am grateful that I was there. He had nightmares mostly about the wars, and how futile most of the fighting and dying was. He talked about how he had to wander through minds that were fanatical in their cause looking for information that would help save lives. He was trying to stop more lives lost. And then finally he talked about the months he had spent in the hospital working his way back after an explosive device blew up too close to his right leg. He says his leg still aches sometimes, but the broken pieces are all put back together."

"We knew nothing of this," admitted Brenna. "I've never treated Kamon, he's never needed me when I've been here. I did find some old injuries when I examined him but they were healed so I didn't ask about them."

"He wouldn't have told you anyway," stated Catherine solemnly. "He's too self-contained. I'm his best friend probably and he never told me either. And due to our childhood pact of not intruding on each other's special gifts, I didn't inquire either."

"He might have shared with Kelly Pierce who had some of the same experiences, but Kelly would never have broken a confidence," asserted Brenna.

"And Kamon did not talk about his trip to California or what happened? No hallucinations about all that either?" asked Brenna.

At Raina's negative nod, Brenna continued, ""So his nightmares or delusions were from the war, not what's happening in the present. Then it seems like he's taking them from his brains long term memory system, rather the short-term one." She was silent for a moment, "That may be a good thing. Matteus's deranged mind may not be a part of anything to do with Kamon."

"As Ione, Kamon's housekeeper says, 'From your mouth to God's ear'." Shifting to a different topic, Raina asked, "Is there anything we can do to help? Anything I can do?"

Brenna cocked her head to one side in thought. "He is close to you even though he fights the connection. I'm guessing that its best that you continue to be who you have become, a grown-up Raina Ramsey. He needs to see and know you for who you are now," she emphasized.

"And don't take any crap from him because of the problems he now has. That would be the worst thing you could do. Pity would shrink his spirit and increase his anger, and neither are good outcomes," Brenna added.

"I agree with Brenna. We all are concerned, but we certainly cannot feel sorry for a vital man like Kamon. And the knowledge of Kamon's disabilities go no further from this room at this time."

Brenna blurted, "But the Council ..."

"The Council will be told when it is necessary to tell them. There's no need to upset the entire clans until we know what we are fighting. That's a command," Catherine did not soften her voice with her two sisters. "If we need help monitoring the situation I will explain it to Sean, Ian, Trent, and Deke. So far, I don't feel that is necessary, so the information stays in this room with just the three of us. Understood?" Again, her voice was strong and forceful.

Both sisters nodded in agreement. Catherine led the clan, including them, and her word was the final one.

"Now tell me about this newcomer," smiled Catherine, speaking to Raina.

"She's telling some truths, some lies, and deliberately omitting answers. Is she a relative of ours? I don't know. I didn't have a chance to talk with her a lot."

"I did as you requested while you were with Kamon," acknowledged Catherine. "I asked Ian and Sean to check some of the story that you both told us. They found records that she was raised by her grandmother under the name of Mary Garcia, and her grandmother did work on the Sandia Indian Reservation as a book-keeper. That checks out. There are no records of her grandmother's past, or for that matter her mother's hospitalization records in Montana when she was young. No death certificate under any name they could find in that time period. Sean thinks she's terrified of something, or someone," mused Catherine.

"She's definitely afraid of something," agreed Raina. "Truthfully, I have very mixed feelings about her. She's pretending to be younger and more innocent than she really is. I hate that. And then deep down I'm not sure I like her very much. That may be my own flaw. I hate being played, and have recently discovered that I also hate subterfuge."

Catherine chewed on her bottom lip, a habit Raina knew she did when deeply troubled. At last she asked Raina, "Would you give it another try? We have to know one way or the other. Kamon is out of danger for now, and there's a host of people who would like to visit with him, but he certainly is not ready to take on an outsider for questioning."

"I think I'll strongly suggest that he remain in his apartment for a couple of days, and then he can pretty much have free rein in the valley after that. Will that work for you two?" asked Brenna.

Catherine and Raina both nodded.

"I do have a problem with Mary Garcia's situation, Catherine. How far do you want me to push her? I'm going to try to be super nice but if that doesn't work ...," Raina let her voice trail off.

"She can't remain anywhere in the valley if she doesn't tell us the whole truth. There's simply too much at stake. Trust is a vital part of our culture and paramount to carrying out our responsibilities. Too many other people would be hurt if she's lying, or even if she's being evasive. If she is not part of our clan system, and has not been taught the ways of our ancestors, then she does not belong here. So far, the only people she has talked to is Alma MacPherson, Sean and you. Correct?"

"Yes. Alma could pass for any well-to-do farmer's wife, and I'm sure that's exactly how she has presented herself. Sean did not talk to her directly at all."

"After you see her, we three will talk again, maybe bring the four men into the conversation to gain outside opinions. And Raina, even if she's connected by a blood ancestor does not mean that she is part of us. Only if she's been raised to respect our ancestors code of honor, is she part of the law."

"I understand, Catherine. I may be able to separate truth from fiction, but I'm glad that the decisions from there are not mine to make," Raina admitted softly smiling in awe at her older sister.

"If a decision has to be made immediately to protect us, then you will make it. Whatever that is. You have the ability and the responsibility. Do you understand?" Catherine said sternly. "Remember your connections and use them."

"I hope it doesn't come to that", mumbled Raina. "Decisions I mean."

"In some ways, the judgements aren't mine to make either, Raina. Over the last two hundred fifty years, our ancestors have had to face many, many different events to protect themselves and the continuance of the clan. They kept meticulous records which Grandmother made us study until we were familiar with the dictates. Thank the Creator for her foresight. Each generation has added information to those records as changing needs have had to be met. We will not be alone in our decisions."

As Raina started to leave the room, Catherine added, "You will know what to do. Trust yourself."

"Are you okay?" asked Sean for the third time as they parked in front of the MacPherson's home.

Raina pulled her thoughts back to the present reluctantly. "I was going over possibilities in my mind," she admitted. "I'm unsure exactly how to approach Mary Garcia. One part of me wants to give her every opportunity to belong here, while another part doesn't want any changes. I think I'm being selfish, but I also know of the importance of being through. What do you think about her, Sean?"

"I don't. I don't have an opinion one way or the other. Checking her background has pointed out large gaps in her story. Raina, that was my job, to do as through a check as was possible with the knowledge she supplied us with. Which was very little, by the way."

"But …,"

"Raina, your job is to separate fact from fiction. You have great instincts for the truth. Use your feelings and that great intuition now. You don't have to separate whatever Mary tells you. The decision you have to make is if what she says is true, or not true. That's it. If she chooses to tell lies, that is not on you. If she chooses to be truthful, that is not on you either. You are not responsible for her actions, only the accuracy of her statements."

"Sean, you are so right! I sometimes forget that I really can't fix the world. Even though I always think I can." She gave him an impulsive hug. "You can be so smart sometimes."

Inside she was smiling. She had been separating fact from fiction by her inner feelings all her life. It was an essential part of her, like breathing air. The connections with the past brought her internal joy. Knowing that she could reach for that internal calmness, and then could use all her senses to know what was true and what was fiction. Grandfather Youngblood had said that all people have the same ability, but especially women. He had taught her to listen to those senses. And he had reminded her that the more she listened to them, the stronger they would become. Now they were an essential part of her. And Kamon needed her to do this job.

Where did that thought come from? Kamon. He was such an essential part of her that even in a crisis he was with her. Was that it? Were they connected in such a way that she could tap into that connection? As soon as she got back she would talk to Catherine about that. With Kamon's lack of romantic interest in her in the past, heartache might be down that road again though. Her attention was jerked back to the present as Sean nudged her arm.

"Hey, I'm always smart, you just don't realize what a gem you have for a bodyguard," he teased.

Raina rolled her eyes in mock exasperation. "Come on, Spock. Let's try to figure this out."

Alma MacPherson greeted them at the door. "Catherine called. Come on in." Alma's greeting was warm and welcoming as always. Raina couldn't read anything into how the last several days had gone with her unexpected guest. Alma would remain neutral to the future of her house guest.

Mary was seated in the great room in an overstuffed sofa with her back to the window. With the light from the window her face was cast in shadows and it would be difficult to read facial expressions or body language. To correct that, Raina took a seat directly next to her. Mary would have to turn sideways to answer her questions.

"Good morning, Mary," Raina greeted cheerfully. Turning to Alma she asked, "Would it be all right if we used the kitchen, Alma? I haven't had coffee today," she explained.

"Good idea," Alma replied smiling. "We all know how you feel about your coffee."

That was the truth. Raina hated the taste of coffee, but she loved the smell. She walked toward the kitchen, flipping on the light switches as she went. Now no one would be in shadow. The rest of the group followed her, Sean seating himself at the head of the table and at an angle from her.

Alma indicated that Mary take the seat across from Raina. "I'll just start the coffee and I do have some of that caramel coffee cake left. It'll just take a minute, you go ahead."

Raina smiled across at the nervous young woman. "I apologize for abandoning you the other day," she said softly. She explained no further.

Mary shrugged, indicating acceptance.

Raina continued speaking not showing how irritated the indifference affected her. "How old are you Mary?"

"Twenty-two."

Raina remained silent. This wasn't going well. Obviously, Mary didn't trust any of them enough to tell the truth. Or maybe the fear overwhelmed her. Whatever the problem, it was not her problem to fix. She was sensitive to nuances, not a psychic. Well, Mary could either start telling them something or not. Both she and Sean had all day. Alma had quietly started fixing snacks to take herself out of the enfolding drama.

Mary sat silently for a couple of minutes, then started to fidget as the silence grew. "Aren't you going to ask me questions?" her tone held a tinge of defiance.

"Nope. Your story is yours to tell, or not."

Mary was silent for several more minutes. Nothing broke the quiet. "My grandmother told me I was twenty-two. I don't have a birth certificate."

Raina remained silent. That much was false. Mary did know if her birth was recorded or not. Not even a driver's license could be applied for without some means of identification.

Mary sat with her eyes downcast and her hands folded in her lap. "I don't know what you want me say."

"Whatever you want to talk about," Raina said softly. She was getting a really bad feeling about Mary being in the valley. Fear was the primary emotion coming off her, and yet she was portraying no apprehension toward the three of them. The dread was coming from inside her. Whatever she feared she had brought with her.

Mary sat with her head down for several more minutes, the only sound was the ticking of the kitchen clock. "You know don't you? she blurted in agitation. "You know I'm hiding out."

"You're hiding out?" asked Raina.

"Yes, damn you. Raymond is going to kill me when he finds me. He said he would and he will," she sobbed holding her hands over her face.

Alma started toward the table, but Raina gave a slight negative nod. "He's going to kill you if he finds you?"

"Yes, I know too much about what he's done; the drugs and, and...."

Raina remained silent.

"I just need to stay here where I'm safe," Mary said sniffling.

"This area is a wild life refuge and a few family farms. There's no town here. Nothing but farms, like this one except smaller. How can we help you?" Raina kept her voice soft and warm.

"There's nothing here but farms? My friend said that the

153

people here were isolated, but he thought they were rich. And I thought there was some kind of town."

Raina forced herself to remain smiling. "Farming doesn't make anyone rich, and there is no town, it's too isolated here. Too few people. And the wild life refuge does not make money."

Mary gave a huge sigh. "That damn fool misled me. Well, hell, I thought I could get a job in town."

Raina leaned forward to engage Mary's eyes. "How can we help you with whatever you're running from?" Mary was a liar, but her fear was real.

Mary's tears were genuine now as they rolled unheeded down her face. "I don't know. Can I go back to being eighteen again and not so stupid?"

Raina smiled ruefully, "Most of us want that. A do-over would be wonderful, but that's not reality. Sometimes the lessons are hard."

"Mine are. I was just so stupid. And young. And stupid," she repeated.

Impulsively Raina asked, "Mary, if you could do what you want, what would that be? What would your future look like?"

"I'd go live with my mom." Tears spilled over at the words.

"Where?"

"In Minnesota near St. Paul. I lied about my mom and dad. My dad died when I was young and my mom and I moved to Albuquerque to live near my grandmother, her mother. Grandma died when I was a sophomore in high school. My other grandparents live on a dairy farm in Minnesota. I did go to school on the Sandia Reservation because Mom worked there, but later I went to an alternative high school in Albuquerque."

She took a deep sigh before continuing. "I thought I knew everything. I gave my mom and grandmother lots of grief, especially my mom. She told me I either had to go to college, or get a job. All I wanted to do was party with my new friends. One thing lead to another, and I ended up in Los Angeles following an Irish band because the drummer was cute. Real, real stupid. After that it was pretty much downhill."

154

"Who are you afraid of now, Mary? The drummer?"

"God, no. Patrick was a great guy, most of the band members were. No, by then I had met Raymond Torres and got mixed up in something deeper. I worked as a waitress. Raymond did drugs and sold drugs whenever he could. He and his friends started selling for a big-time drug dealer and thought they were really smart."

She hid her head in her hands. "I ran because they said that I had to pull my own weight, and go to parties with them. I knew those parties were drug houses with sex for sale, and a lot of underage girls. I told him that I didn't want to do that kind of thing, and that I wanted to leave. Raymond told me that another guy's girlfriend had tried to run off, and the guy had beaten her so badly that she ended up in the hospital. I don't know what happened to her after that."

All true so far, Raina noted. Mary wasn't playing games anymore; she was too terrified.

"For once I got lucky. This long-distance haul truck driver I knew from the diner said he would give me a ride to Albuquerque after I told him what Raymond was planning to do. He refused to get involved, but made an anonymous phone call to the police from a throw-away phone."

Still true, thought Raina. m

"When I got back to Albuquerque, I didn't know anyone. I had been gone four years and all my friends had moved on with their lives, and my mom was gone. I went to see Angie Apodaca at the reservation, and she told me that my mom had moved back to Minnesota. That's where she had grown up, and where my dad's parents lived. Then one of the women from the band group called me and told me that Raymond was looking for me, and he was really angry. He knew my home was in Albuquerque, so I figured it was a question of time before he found me."

"Why here?" asked Raina softly. She wanted to keep her talking. She forced herself to be sedate which was not her normal persona.

"Tamal told me about this place. Tamal was one of the

guys who sold drugs with Raymond and had done time. He got drunk one night and started telling prison stories, and how each prisoner had tried to tell the most outlandish exploits of what they had done."

"Anyway, he said that some Irish prisoner had talked about this rich place in Arkansas that was in the hills. He said that no one believed him, they all told lies to make themselves look smarter and meaner. Anyway, the guy told Tamal the next day that it was the truth, and told him about where it was located. I did believe it. Besides I had nothing to lose. Anywhere was better than where Raymond could find me."

"Is your mom's still in Minnesota? Have you had any contact with her?" Raina left the question open-ended.

"No. Haven't seen or heard from her since I ran away. She probably hates me," Mary said breaking into sobs again.

"What's your real name? Do you have identification, like a driver's license?" An idea was starting to come together in Raina's mind.

"It's Mary. Mary Garcia Gunderson. And I do have a driver's license from California. It's under the name of Gunderson although everyone thought my last name was Garcia. I had to drive to work sometimes, although mostly Raymond drove me."

"Do you want to go to Minnesota? To be with your family?"

"More than anything, but they might not want me. And I'll need to work and save some money first. I was so stupid to believe all the crap they said. Young and stupid."

"Water under the bridge, as my grandfather would say." Raina turned to Sean and Alma who had been silently listening. "I could pitch in some money if you two could help. I don't have much from my last paycheck. Maybe we could help her buy an airplane ticket home to Minnesota?"

Neither Alma or Sean allowed shock to show on their faces. Money was never a problem for the Ramsey's or their clans. Investments would keep them more than solvent forevermore.

Sean spoke first. "I have a little money from my job. I could contribute a little if it will help."

"Me too," said Alma quickly. "Not much, but if we pool our money it should be enough."

"Good," Raina nodded fighting a grin. "Is that what you want to do Mary?" At Mary's tearful affirmative nod, Raina continued, "What about the car you're driving?"

"You really mean it? I'll pay you back, honest I will. I've learned my lesson and I want to be a normal good person like my mother. Oh, I bought the car from a junk yard in New Mexico. The pink slip is in the glove compartment; I could sign it. If it's alright, I could donate it to a rescue mission or something. Or you could maybe sell it and get a little of your money back."

"Okay, then let's plan. Mary, you drive to the airport in Spring Creek. Do you know where that is?"

"Yes, beside the hospital on the other edge of the town. I came in that way."

"Leave the car at the airport, keys under the passenger mat. We will leave a paid ticket for you waiting there. Alma will take you back to the road you came in on, then it's a straight shot to Spring Creek. To be on the safe side, use back streets to the airport, and keep as low a profile as possible."

"If I can have your address I will pay you back. Honest I will. It might take awhile, but I'll repay every cent," Mary said sincerely, her face wet with tears.

There were no addresses in Shadow Valley, no postal services and never had been. That would have put them on the map, and thus on other people's radar. All paper correspondence now was either through New York attorneys, or a private arrangement through the Gowan family businesses in Exeter. The easiest explanation was often the simplest though.

"Thank you so much for your offer, Mary. We appreciate it. But instead of repaying us, how about helping someone else that needs help? Pass it on and tell whoever you help to pass it on and on down the line. That way all the bad stuff that's happened to you has a good ending."

Raina glanced at Sean to see if he had anything to add to her improvised suggestion. He gave a slight nod of approval.

"I promise," gushed Mary. "I know other people need stuff too, so I'll do that. I don't know what my momma will say when I see her, but whatever it is I deserve it. And I'll prove myself to her, and to my dad's family."

"I think you will too. Good luck," Raina said sincerely, standing up to give Mary a hug.

Mary quickly packed her meager supply of clothes, gave Raina a warm hug, and thanked her again. She even gave Sean a hug and a soft thank you. She was still saying thank you and waving frantically as she drove off, following Alma's farm truck.

"You done good," Sean smiled broadly, giving Raina's arm a pat. "Kamon couldn't have done a better job. He's not nearly as creative. I'm proud of you," he grinned.

"Thanks, the only other thing is for you to remind me to tell Catherine about a couple of things. First the car needs to be dismantled so it's untraceable, and this ex-con band member, Tamal, needs to be checked out. Just to be on the safe side, he needs checking out by MAC."

CHAPTER NINETEEN

"Good job, Raina," praised Catherine.

Catherine was seated in one of the reclining chairs in Kamon's sitting room with her, surrounded by Sean, Liam, Brenna, Deke, Kamon and Trent. Catherine's four-year-old daughter was playing with her young cousin, Brandon, underneath Kamon's desk. Catherine had just finished telling Kamon about the outsider that had entered their valley, and the details of how Raina, Sean, and Alma had handled it.

Kamon smiled softly at Raina. Damn, even with that shaggy brown hair, she's beautiful. And she had handled the situation extremely well with no input from anyone else. In a very grown-up thoughtful way, leaving the intruder girl with her pride intact, but protecting the valley too.

"You did do a very good job, Raina. Probably better than I would have done," he admitted. "I'm not nearly as tactful as you are. Or as pretty."

Stunned silence. All eyes went back and forth between Raina and Kamon.

Gathering herself together with a pounding heart, Raina tried for cool. "Thank you. Truthfully, I did my best to imagine what you would do and went for it."

She smiled at him, all the time trying to maintain some coherent thought, her heart beating frantically. In all the years she had know him, Kamon had never complimented her on her personal attributes. Hell, most of the time he didn't praise her for anything she did, period.

The ensuring silence was broken by Catherine asking Raina, "Do you think that Mary believed you about this being a few isolated farms? And is that the last of it?"

Raina pulled back her thoughts from Kamon reluctantly. "Yes, I think so. I hope we played it really low key enough for her not to want to ever come back. Alma MacPherson was a wonder, nice but neutral. Not aiming for best friends, but helping Mary a little. Sean said very little as we had agreed upon. Sean, what do you think? Will Mary come back, or will there be other repercussions?"

"I don't think so. I checked, and she did exactly as you instructed, drove to Spring Creek, left the car there, and picked up her economy airplane ticket. Sitting in the cheapest seat in the back row. I think she's going to have her hands so full when she gets to Minnesota, explaining her life for the last four years that she will forget us. By the way, it was brilliant to have her pass our good deed on to someone else. That too will make her forget us. I'll check her social media sites for awhile just to make sure though."

"And I've called MAC to have them do a check on this Tamal man she mentioned," added Catherine.

"Then everything is back to normal?" asked Trent. "Well, except for the fact that our son will be born in a month or so." Trent was overtly thrilled with his increasing family. A businessman who spent less and less time at his office in New York City, he doted on his wife, fretted over her pregnancy, and spoiled their daughter shamelessly.

Catherine shook her head in mock exasperation. "I wish," she murmured softly.

"Which brings the conversation back to what I asked you all to met here for," said Kamon with a deep sigh. "As you can know, the Kunjin virus has made me tire more easily. Brenna says that pesky mosquito laid me low for awhile. And she has my thanks for all her help," Kamon smiled at Brenna in appreciation. "But I need to tell you all something else."

"You're sure you want to do this?" Catherine asked. "You know you don't have to. We could just wait to see."

"Yes, I need to tell everyone here." Looking at each member

of the group, his eyes rested on Raina. "Most of you know parts of what happened with the prisoner in California, but I need to tell you all of it." He blew out a deep breath. "I Mind Walked through a madman's brain for information on a possible prison break. The first time, I gained needed information of some men kidnapping a bunch of young girls for some very ugly purpose. MAC and others took care of that. During interrogations, we gained information about a possible prison break and mass killings led by the same madman."

He paused to allow everyone to absorb that information. "The second time I Walked, I had to enter into a section of the brain where planning takes place. The prisoner somehow sensed something was wrong, and went totally berserk, falling completely into madness. A violent, insane psychopath. Long story, but the part that is important is that I might not have gotten my own mind out in time. I may have taken some, or all, of his insanity with me."

Again he stopped. "Neither Brenna nor Catherine think that happened, but I will not allow anyone to bond with me to check that out, neither physically or mentally. Our edits are very clear on the unborn. I agree with them that I probably got out of his brain in time before he became a raving manic. The symptoms of insanity would have manifested itself almost immediately. But I wanted you all to know about it. And continue to monitor me for it."

When Liam started to say something, Kamon held up his hand in the stop mode. "Unfortunately there's more."

The room was quiet, even the little kids playing under the desk were silent.

"I may no longer have the gift as a Mind Walker, a telepath."

"How do you know?" asked the ever pragmatic Deke Paxton.

"Now, an even harder part to admit." He talked directly to Raina. "There has always been a connection between us, Raina. A bonding. An unbroken spiritual awareness since you were very young. Even when I pushed hard to sever it, it remained.

161

When we were at Deke and Brenna's ranch, and I first regained consciousness, I could no longer feel that completeness. I don't know exactly how to explain it, but it was like looking down and finding my right arm missing. There was an empty sensation of loss and bereavement. I could no longer feel that connection. The link was broken between us. We were not connected."

Raina stared back at him. Should she tell him? She had to, even though it would hurt him initially, she was honor-bound to tell him. He needed the information more than he needed to be protected.

"Since you were so honest with me, I'll tell you what happened. It had nothing to do with your ability to Mind Walk. A lifetime ago before I left here, I felt different toward you. I felt joined also. Then it became no longer true for me."

She nibbled on her lower lip trying to find the words to say. "In Texas, I blocked you from my being. I have that ability. I didn't want to connect with you so I prevented the link between us. My choice." This time there was unaccustomed steel in her voice. "I chose."

Kamon closed his eyes to shield his overwhelming emotions. Then he didn't know if his gift was lost or not. Maybe he was still okay. Still able to help those who needed his gift. She had deliberately blocked him from her mind. During the time Raina had been gone, she had become stronger. The woman she was meant to become.

Raina now had enough internal power to block anyone. Even him. And she did have the right to choose. The pain he felt at the words took his breathe away, into his very substance. He had lost her.

No, he had not lost her, because he had never had her, not really. He had never allowed her to know him, and to become a part of him. And now could never be. Not this incredible creature she had grown into.

"Then you don't know if you can connect with anyone or not," Brenna said thoughtfully, getting to the real issue. "And if somehow you can no longer Mind Walk, that really doesn't make a tremendous difference now. It simply means you can no longer Mind Walk. You're still Kamon Youngblood. You're still Catherine's ceaan-cath, Sgnoch Council member, and cousin to us all. And we still love you."

"True, although I do know that you would feel that a part of you is missing, Kamon," added Catherine. "You also know the edits and rules of our ancestors. They taught us that whether a person has a unique gift or does not, that they are no less of value than the gifted ones. None of our little ones are gifted, yet they are all precious."

"Then let's find out," Raina stared directly at Kamon. "I'm neither pregnant, nor will I block you from my mind if you're willing to try to connect with me. Try to connect with me, please, Kamon. Then you will know for sure."

"No. Absolutely not. I would never chance that there's something I don't know about my own brain. That I could pass whatever on to you. The risk is too great. I can't do it. I will not do it."

"Kamon's right. It is too soon. Let his body and mind heal, and then we may have more information we can use." Brenna suggested.

"My Daddy likes 'formation," stated Alexa with her four-year-old authority. "He's always asking people for more. And more. And more, mama says." Alexa had climbed up on her father's lap listening when the adults were unaware.

"Out of the mouths of babes," Brenna quoted, grinning at Trent. Trent was famous for his need to gather as much information as possible on whatever subject he was working on. To the point of ad nauseam.

"Brandon got tired and went to sleep," Alexa explained, leaning her head on her father's chest.

A smiling Deke hunkered down in front of the keyhole in the desk. Brandon lay sprawled out asleep like a giant relaxed frog, drool seeping from his slack mouth. Deke carefully picked him up cradling him in his arms, oblivious of the wet spot now on his shirt. Brandon didn't stir.

Kamon smiled as Deke and Brenna exchanged warm glances. Brandon was a constant source of joy and wonder for two people who had never expected to have a family. And his own heart ached with envy. Deke had almost lost his life, and Brenna had saved it. Now they melded into two people who shared everything.

Not for the first time, he admitted he wanted that. Maybe he didn't deserve it. Hell, he knew he didn't, but coming so close to death and insanity revised much of his feelings. He felt Raina looking at him, her head cocked to one side in thought.

Raina. A grown up Raina. Young, but tough enough to be his equal in all things. She would never take any crap from him, or anyone else. And Raina was the one person that completed him. That made him whole. Not just as a man, although truthfully she made his heart pound and his jeans bulge, but her spirit. The spirit that said a lifetime of commitment or nothing. This would not be like all the other woman before. Was it possible that he had been wrong. That they could ever be a couple? To have what Deke and Brenna had?

Truthfully, he did not know this grown up Raina, her likes and dislikes. How changed she had become. Or if there was a chance in hell of her still having feelings for him. But now that was the most important thing in the world for him to explore. He had always been a risk taker and the idea that Raina could develop feelings for him again made his palms sweat.

Raina, the sprite, the imp that had hovered in the back of his mind forever.

"I need to run something by you, Raina." Kamon kept his voice neutral. "Do you have some time this morning?"

All eyes stared at him. Brenna's eyebrows went up in question. Kamon chuckled to himself. The Mama Bear trait. Brenna was the closest in age to Raina with a ten-year age difference, but she had often played with her when she was very young. Later she had been the big sister that Raina had sought out with her childhood tears.

Catherine and their grandmother had such huge responsibilities that the two younger girls were left mostly to other people's care. That the care had been warm, loving and kind was still not the same as having a mother-father family unit who loved each other. He knew that.

"Sure, Kamon," Raina's voice was quiet and indifferent. "I have some time. Sean and I were going to go out to Sanhicks to look over that new generator that came in. It can wait. Okay, Sean?"

"Do you want me to wait for you?" Sean asked, keeping his voice neutral with difficulty. Protecting Raina was his duty, not only her physical person, but her emotional wellbeing. But here in the valley, she called her own shots.

"That's all right, I'll go out later this afternoon or tomorrow," Raina said offhandedly. "Unless there's something super exciting happening, then you better call me," she instructed firmly, narrowing her eyes.

Liam and Sean walked out of the room but not before Sean gave Raina a quiet 'I hope you know what you're doing' look.

CHAPTER TWENTY

"I'm not really sure there's something specific I want to talk to you about," admitted Kamon, after everyone left the room. "I do want you to know what a good job with Mary you did. Truthfully, I would not have been nearly as tactful. Or as creative. Having her pass the good deed on was inspirational."

"Thank you." Raina remained quiet. Wherever this conversation was going, it was on him. She no longer had the responsibility of making him happy, she never had but hadn't known it. Now she did. She wouldn't be rude, but her job of adoration was done.

Unfortunately, one part of her wanted to be that starstruck teen of the past worshiping Kamon. That was comforting in some ways, redoing the same experience over and over, knowing how he would react. The other part of her wanted to say hell no. Never. Too much giving and not enough getting hurt too much. The hell no, never, won.

"Tell me about your adventures," Kamon coaxed softly. "What was your favorite part of the country? And what was your favorite thing that happened? I know you can't tell me all of them but what are some of the best ones?"

"Really, mostly we traveled from Oklahoma, Texas, Arizona and then to California," she explained without going into any details.

"Did you sightsee? Was that your purpose?" Kamon asked.

"Yes and no. We did sightsee, but we also spent time with the people we met."

Kamon was quiet for a couple of minutes, then heaved a long sigh. "Raina, I'm basically a simple man, and I know I'm too hard and rigid. But the premise of destructive and constructive values is what I have tried to live by. Destructive has potentially bad results and constructive good ones. Simple, most of the time that's effective, and something I can live with."

"Somehow, I've messed that up between us. I'm sorry Raina. For whatever I did. You're much the same person with the family as you were before you left. Only with me are you different. Very different. Are you willing to tell me whatever it was that I said, so I can apologize?" his voice pleaded gently.

"No. I'm not willing to discuss it. But I do accept your apology." She sat straighter in her chair. Kamon apologizing was a first step and one she had not expected. "And our trip was interesting."

"How so?" asked Kamon, willing to take whatever she was willing to give.

Thinking back over the last several months, Raina answered truthfully. "Each state held different experiences. In Oklahoma, the experience of organizing a large area of debris into areas that were manageable was probably a highlight. And spending time with Brandon," she grinned, remembering the antics of the toddler.

"Near San Antonio, Texas, we worked at a shelter as Catherine had requested, and I learned so much. There were so many people who had become homeless through no fault of their own. With my limited knowledge, I had thought that the people in the shelters would be addicts, or all of them to have mental health issues. That was simply not true. I found that many people live one paycheck from being homeless."

"I found the same thing, even in other countries," admitted Kamon.

"It's really sad. There was this one young woman who had a little baby. Her family was horrified that she had gotten pregnant, and had kicked her out of their home. The father of the child was long gone. She had no place to go and no other resources. She lived at the shelter for months, helping as much as she could with cooking and serving meals to other people who were homeless. Anyway, with a little help the shelter was able to hook her up with some social service resources and get her into a little apartment, a tiny efficiency. The social worker will help her finish high school and get her life in order with some medical help." She shook her head in wonder. "You would have thought she had been given a pot of gold."

Kamon smiled at the animated face. It was lit from within like a primary light source. "And you and Sean helped the shelter with those extra resources, right? Anonymously of course." When Raina nodded, Kamon asked "Where did you go next?"

"We wandered around for awhile in little towns, then went to New Mexico, the Land of Enchantment. I could so live there, although I admit I said the same thing about San Antonio. We volunteered at a Catholic pre-school for low income families, and worked at odd jobs using a barter system. And we saw Albuquerque which is awesome, especially Old Town. A tri-cultural city. I loved it."

"White, Mexican, and Native American?" asked Kamon? "Strangely, I've never been there."

"Some who classify themselves as Mexican, but many say they are Spanish. Their ancestors were from Spain, not Mexico. The capital, Santa Fe, is the oldest capitol in the United States. And the only city that has been under five different governments. Something they are very proud of."

"I'd forgotten that, if I ever knew it," grinned Kamon. "Then Arizona?" Kamon prompted. He loved to hear the sound of her voice. It sent a low hum throughout his body spreading warmth. He wanted to keep her talking for days. And talking to her now was unlike anything he had ever experienced. She was smart, funny, and effervescent. She loved life and it loved her right back.

The following week allowed everyone to get back into the rhythm of work and their normal routine. Kamon asked Raina to spend as much time with him as she could. Always adding, "Only if you choose. It's no longer an order. I do not have the right to order you anymore except in my role as ceann-cath."

Raina had laughed and retorted, "Well, that's different. But in truth Kamon, I like to talk with you. You actually listen now. It's a dialogue, not a lecture."

At first they had talked mostly about her travels in the Southwest. He asked her about people she had met on their wanderings and how she felt about each experience. She told him about Joe, an Air Force veteran, and his struggles with addition. And about Suzi, the retired teacher who spent everyday volunteering somewhere "to make it better for someone". And the tiny preschooler who asked her if her facial 'scar' hurt and did she want him to kiss it?

And finally, she told him about Juana, a young twentyish Hispanic woman that she had met serving breakfast at a food kitchen. Juana had contracted leukemia in elementary school. She knew she was on borrowed time and yet she lived life fully. Juana told her of work in a foster care non-profit, and of her volunteering with a medical group helping street people. And finally of her plans to go home to her family to spend what she knew would be her last days with her parents and other loved ones as they requested. Raina felt tears gather in her eyes as she told Kamon how Juana had hugged her and Sean when they left, and told them she'd wait for them on the other side.

They talked about the way each experience affected her, and how closely Sean had guarded her without stifling her. Kamon admitted that he was envious of all she had done and experienced on their awanderin'.

He had laughed when she told him about all the antics of the preschoolers in Albuquerque and the necessity of watching them every minute. "Turn your back for an instant and something happens, even if it's only one of them playing 'shower' with dirt raining down on everyone."

Raina enjoyed her time with Kamon but after several weeks, there didn't seem to be any movement toward taking their relationship to another level. She had to know if she was still wasting her time on someone inaccessible, or if Kamon and their friendship was going in the new direction it had seemed to be at first. The only way she knew was to confront the issue head on.

She went to see her big sister, clan leader and sister, Catherine Ramsey.

"Catherine, I need your help," Raina said bluntly. "Kamon and I have spent lots of time together over the last weeks. I feel that I know him better and yet in some ways, I really don't. He wants to spend time talking about me, but not sharing about himself. Before, I never made any secret of my youthful adoration of him. I've apologized for making him uncomfortable with my cloying craziness."

"Now I've hit a brick wall. I feel like I'm running in place and going nowhere. So far and no farther. He seems to want to be with me as much as I'm willing. Catherine, I've been willing to spend lots of time just talking. But now .... I'm frustrated. I want more. I want to know that this new relationship is going to amount to something, or if he's just bored and I'm available to spend time with."

Catherine was serious as she answered, "I do agree with you. You've finished all the education you've wanted, and you've lived outside the valley. You've seen and experienced other ways of life. Grandmother said you were born old, that you have an old soul. And now you're restless. At this point in your life you can go anywhere and be anything you wish."

"Maybe travel and help Marie in Paris. Or volunteer for the Aid Organization," Raina said thoughtfully.

"Those are always options. Travel is always an education, but as you discovered, you do take your problems with you. For now, why don't you give it a few more days. Think about it some more."

"Yeah, you're right. I'm frustrated and that makes me angry," Rain grinned wryly. "I think I'll go for a horseback ride. Fergus has this new mare, Starlight, that I've been riding every day."

Two hours later, Catherine knocked on Kamon's office door next to her own office in the Stone House. "Hey, Kamon."

"Good Morning, Catherine. What brings you out this very

fine day?" Kamon grinned in good humor. Spending time with Raina made his heart sing and gave a spring to each step. Even dealing with the many problems of the tribal clan Council was easier somehow.

"I have a problem and I thought I would share it with you. Mayhap you can help."

"Sure, I'd be glad to listen. You know, I'm always available to you as your ceann cath, and as your friend."

Catherine nibbled her lower lip in thought. "Well, there is this situation where a young woman is trying to make a next-step decision in her life. A decision that may have long term consequences."

Kamon sat straighter in his chair, immediately wondering if she was talking about Raina or someone else. "Are you willing to share the name of this young woman?" he asked his heart pounding, and all his senses alert.

"For now, no. She's trying to decide if she should stay in a situation where she's frustrated and thinks she's spinning her wheels, or to move on to someone and someplace else." Catherine held his gaze without blinking. "And she does have choices."

Kamon barely breathed as he asked the most basic question, "Why is she frustrated?"

"It seems that her sharing in a particular relationship goes only one way, and she's doing all the sharing. And you know that without mutual sharing, there can be no intimacy. Without intimacy, the relationship becomes stagnant. And many times the relationship ceases altogether."

Kamon sat in stunned silence. Raina. And his deficiencies and denials. His lack of ability to share his inner self. His thoughts but mostly his feelings. "I truly do not know what to say to you, Catherine. I'm at a loss."

"It's actually pretty simple. This young lady is at a cross-roads. One has her leaving our area, maybe permanently. More than likely out of the United States. If the choice is the other road, she needs to feel that disclosures are not a one-way street. That there is a building toward a future here. Your choice," she touched his shoulder gently as she left the room.

Choice? There was no choice. Raina's leaving and possibly finding a mate would kill all feelings inside him. He wouldn't be just empty inside; he would be dead instead. There would be nothing for him, no hope or satisfaction in anything he did. And just maybe, there was an outside chance that some of her feelings for him would remain intact after he told her.

Again then, no choice. The pain of losing her against the pain of telling her. No choice.

CHAPTER TWENTY-ONE

"Raina, this is Kamon. I need to talk to you about something. Could you please come to my office?"

"Sure, Kamon. I'm at Fergus's stables. I'll be there as soon as I put up Starlight. Is there anything wrong?"

"Yes and no. I'll explain when you get here. I'm at my Stone House office."

Kamon gathered his thoughts together, trying to rehearse the best way to tell Raina about who he was, and why. After mulling over the best way to tell her about himself, he decided that the unblemished truth was probably best. She would either look down on him with horror, or accept the man he had become.

"You wanted to see me?" asked Raina entering the office and taking the seat nearest his own chair.

Kamon closed the door behind her, and returned to his own seat before answering her. In truth he wished he could lock the door and force her to stay. Just to stay.

"Raina, do you believe in Karma? That we pay for what we've done? Good or evil?"

Raina's answer was slow in coming. "I'm unsure exactly how it works, but I believe in a Destiny. But I also think that we have choices in what we do. Do you believe in Karma, is that what you wanted to ask?"

"I probably do not believe in the same way you mean it, but I believe in a directed Karma."

"I don't know what a directed Karma is. To me, those words seem oppositional."

"You know I was raised by Grandfather Youngblood who was close to the spirit world his entire life." She gave a nod in agreement, knowing the truth of the statement. "As you know he taught me the belief system he had, and that had been passed down to him."

"And you were very, very lucky," Raina said wistfully, as she lapsed into silence.

Instead he answered, "I was. But I also had a life before Grandfather Youngblood. Before Shadow Valley. I need to tell you of my own background before I can have a relationship. And I want one. With you. A forevermore relationship."

He could hear her swift intake of breath, but doggedly continued. "Please don't interrupt because this is incredibly difficult for me."

Raina nodded in acquiesce, eyes wide and serious.

"My first complete memory was when I was four or five years old. Before that I only remember bits and pieces of my early life. My mother was Native American, and my father was a white man. From pieces of my memory, my mother must have been very young, and my father was only a few years older. He told me once that she had just started high school when they ran away together. She was pregnant with me."

He paused for a moment. "Later I figured out that she went into early labor somewhere, and without a doctor, she died. My father was immature, easily led, and had no work skills."

"One of my first real memories is of sitting on an old sofa with my father. He and a bunch of his friends were really drunk and noisy. I must have been about four years old. I told my father that the cops were going to come and arrest people. He didn't believe me, but the cops did come. One of his friends, a guy named Jimmy, asked me how I knew and I shrugged my shoulders. He hit me across the face, but I couldn't tell him because I didn't know how I knew. My dad's current girl friend told them I had probably guessed, but I hadn't. Much later I figured out that I had gotten the vibe from one of the people there. She had called the cops."

Kamon watched as Raina listened to him, her face interested and sad. Throwing all the chips in the game took all the courage he had.

"Things went down hill pretty much after that. My father's drug habit increased, and his friends became sleazier and more corrupt. They started stealing. They stole from the people in the neighborhood, then low key burglaries in the area."

"They started asking me if there was anyone home at such and such a house. Sometimes I knew, and sometimes I didn't know. At first, I said I didn't know, but they learned that a beating brought about an answer if there was one. I pretty much stayed a mass of bruises. Sometimes they would withhold food if they thought I should know. And I had never been taught much of anything. No rights. No wrongs."

Fat tears rolled silently down Raina's face.

Kamon continued doggedly on, wanting to finish. "They started robbing convenience stores, mostly small mom and pop kind of operations. I told them that a particular convenience store had never been robbed, because the owner had a gun underneath the counter."

"Of course, those stupid druggies decided that they would rob it since no one else had ever succeeded. The owner killed my father, and two of the others including Jimmy." He took a deep breath to steady himself and continued.

"Glenda, the lady we were living with at the time, was hard-core and wanted nothing to do with a little kid. She told me she was moving back to New York. That wasn't the truth, she was moving to Los Angeles. Anyway, she put what clothes I had in a paper bag, and drove me about 40 miles out of Albuquerque to a pueblo village on a reservation. She stopped at a side road within sight of some adobe structures, told me to get out, and she drove away."

"I remember just standing there, having no idea what to do. I couldn't read or write, and had never been to school. I knew my first name was Kamon, but I had used at least five different last names and didn't know my real one. No birth certificate."

Kamon glanced at Raina. Her eyes were closed, but tears seeped between her lashes. She was biting her lip as if to keep from crying out.

"An old woman saw me from her window and came to get me. And she talked to me. Not at me, but to me. Like I was a real person. I told her the truth about my life, and that I could tell her what she was thinking. I told her that she was thinking of calling the tribal police, but instead was going to call her brother. She called him, then fed me posole and beans with corn bread. As much as I wanted, then chocolate cake. It was the best meal of my life. I can still remember the taste of the peppers."

Kamon swallowed, going on with his story. "An old man in a pickup truck came when it was just getting dark. They put me in the front seat of the truck and covered me with blankets. That old woman kissed the top of my head. I had never been kissed before and it made my heart ache."

He continued, wanting to get it all out, needing for her to know. "We drove for an hour or two. I can't remember exactly how long because I slept. Anyway, we drove out in the desert, and when I woke up, we had stopped at an old asphalt road. An airplane was there. The pilot and another man bundled me up in some blankets to keep me warm and we took off. When I woke again, we were landing in a tiny airport in the mountains. Later, I realized that the airport was Sanhicks, here in Shadow Valley."

"A Native American man came to talk to me. He asked me all kinds of question, and I first tried to lie. He told me not to lie and that he knew when I did. He said he knew that I could see into other people's minds. I asked him who he was. He told me he was my grandfather, and was called Grandfather Youngblood. He told me my name was Kamon Youngblood, and I would be living with him and Grandmother Youngblood for the rest of my life."

He blinked to hide the emotion. "And he said that they loved me. I burst into tears, the only happy tears I had ever shed up to that point in my life. At last someone who wanted who, and what, I was. Someone who saw me as a person and still loved me. I had value."

Kamon was quiet for a couple of minutes, wanting to be

sure he had told Raina everything. When she started to speak, he held up his hand to stop her.

"I need to tell you everything while I can. Few people knew that Grandfather Youngblood occasionally helped MAC, the clandestine operatives. As you know Grandfather did not Mind Walk, but he was deeply intuitive and read body language. They only asked Grandfather when there were no other options."

"When I was about seventeen, Grandmother Youngblood was diagnosed with an aggressive form of leukemia. So, when MAC came calling, Grandfather Youngblood said he couldn't go. The situation was to gain information from a corrupt official regarding young children working in Bangladesh. I asked if I could go instead of Grandfather."

Again he paused, "Long story short, I became deeply involved in MAC. I had seen so much brutality in my early childhood that few things bothered me."

He took a deep breath and exhaled slowly. "Raina, I'm not a good man, and I will never be. It is not who I am. Killing bad guys that need to be killed does not bother my conscience. If I have one. I work less now for MAC but with Catherine's permission, I still do things for MAC that would make you cringe. Or vomit."

"I have Walked through minds that are deranged, filthy, and immoral beyond your imagination. Brenna says that Matteus did not transfer his madness to me, but we still do not know if I have my ability to Mind Walk since the episode with him. That may be gone."

Raina wiped the tears away, looking at Kamon in a new light, her eyes shining. "Kamon, you are a soldier. In some ways you are not a bad man or a good man. You are a modern-day warrior. There's no other way to say it. You are as people have contributed to your being. No, you will never be mind-mannered, maybe never behave in what some would call gentlemanly. That's not your Destiny."

She took a deep breath and said honestly, "Kamon, I don't need that. I need the man who is you. During your fever battles, you told me all about your war years. What you did, how you felt. And about your wounds, physically and emotionally. I hurt for you but nothing you have done repels me. As to your beginnings, you were a vulnerable child. Period."

"Raina, I want you to be very, very sure. I'm a completely selfish man. If I have you, nothing will ever take you away from me. Nothing." He straightened to his full height. "I want you to take time to process all this. For me, you are perfect, untouched by the dark places in my life. I've always thought of you as shimmering sunlight. Shadow Valley's sunshine."

"Raina, you are my dream, a dream I thought I could never have. I hope you understand why I've avoided telling you all this. We'll talk in the morning again if you still want to pursue a permanent us," Kamon said quietly as he walked out.

Raina tried in vain to blink back the tears as Kamon left. She shed tears over the lost little boy no one wanted. She cried for the manipulation of a child and the vulnerabilities his own father had taken advantage of. The little boy who never had the love he needed in his life before he met Grandfather Youngblood.

And she wept for the Kamon who needed and wanted to belong, even if he didn't know it, or know he needed it.

She knew she could never wait until tomorrow to see him. To tell him that all he had become was perfect for her. Without his past he wouldn't be the man he was; self-contained, raw and real. And she wanted all of him, the overwhelmingly masculine warrior with facial scars. The leader who understood what pain was because he had lived it. The helper who aided those who were as vulnerable as he once had been. Kamon was not easy, and would probably never be. Warriors never were.

She ran out of the room, down the stairs and back to the stables to saddle Starlight. She waved at Fergus as she rode out of the meadow, taking a short cut to Kamon's house. Her mind was in a turmoil, going over what he had endured and the strength it had taken to overcome it.

She had been so angry with him, so hurt over his liaison with the woman in Spring Creek. Now it seemed like a childish reaction to a man that felt he was unworthy of a permanent bonding. She had wanted Kamon to say and do exactly what she wanted him to do. To feel what she wanted him to feel. Now she could at least partially understand the whys of some of his reactions. She needed to tell him of her feelings now, not in the morning.

The feral pigs took her by complete surprise. Unfortunately, Starlight was in the herd of swine before she could turn him around. One wild pig gored Starlight's right flank as they all started to attack his legs and hindquarters. Starlight panicked, bucking as he tried to avoid the tusks of the wild pigs.

Raina grabbed a limb from a nearby tree, and raised herself off the saddle before her horse could buck her off. Relieved of her weight, Starlight kicked out and ran, some of the wild pigs pursuing her as she raced down the path.

The limb that Raina had grabbed onto was a low hanging branch of a young sapling. She climbed as high as could without bending the young tree. Immediately the largest wild sow started banging her head against the little tree to bring the tree down. Raina knew that it was just a question of time before that was an eventuality.

She hadn't brought her phone with her and had no way of getting help. There might be a chance that Starlight would make it back to the stables, someone would see she was hurt and hunt for her. Slim chance though.

She closed her eyes and yelled in her mind, "Help, Kamon. Help." She concentrated all of her being into sending Kamon the message that she needed him. He may, or may not, hear her. The connection between them was strong but Mind Walking required proximity. All she could do was try to reach him. And he may no longer have the gift of Walking now at all.

"Kamon, help! Kamon, please hear me. Help!" Raina's voice was clear and terrified. Kamon was disoriented for a moment as he realized that Raina's voice was in his head. He tried to send her a message asking where she was, but there was only an ominous silence.

He could still Mind Walk. He could hear her desperate shout

179

of needing help but did not know where she could be. What a time to admit the depth of the love he had for the sunshine of his life. A time to know that if the choice ever was Raina or anything else, Mind Walking or even himself, he would choose Raina first. Always Raina first.

Beginning to panic himself as he continued unsuccessfully to reach her with his mind, he called Catherine asking her to check Raina's room to see if she was there. He told Catherine about the message in his head and that wherever Raina was, she needed help. After a few moments, Catherine returned to say no she wasn't anywhere in the Stone House. He drove quickly to the Stone House for information and to organize a search. Catherine, Trent, Deke, Brenna, Sean, and Ian met him by the stables.

Fergus told them that Raina had waved as she took the shortcut to a path that would lead her to Kamon's house. A bleeding Starlight had returned to the stables moments before, frightened and bleeding. Fergus showed them the cuts on Starlight's legs and flanks. "Ken from a pig" he told them as he examined Starlight's wounds.

"Fergus, would you stay here to treat Starlight with me," asked Brenna. At his dark frown, she added, "Please Fergus. I know you want to go too, but I'm not sure I can handle Starlight by myself and those cuts need stiches."

Fergus's nod was quick and surly.

Kamon started a rapid jog as he began to track the horse's mad dash through the thick woods. Trent, Deke, Sean, and Liam followed him at the same punishing pace. Kamon knew that the four other men could keep up the fast rate as they had all been through the Warrior Society training. That hundreds year old vow given by the Society to be the Swords and Shields to protect the women with the unique gifts handed down by ancestors' eons ago.

After a couple of miles of running, Kamon slowed as he heard the grunting and snorting of the feral swine. Each man slowed then stopped as they waited for Kamon, the ceann cath, to make the next decision. Kamon raised a hand to indicate moving in a small fan grouping as they walked quickly toward the small clearing. Raina could be seen clinging to a small sapling while a giant feral pig waited at the bottom. The bark on the tree had been peeled back as if the pig had hit it multiple times.

"I'll get the old sow. If the others don't run, then they too have to be shot," he told the other men. Raising his rifle, he shot the sow through the head. She dropped instantly. With the noise of the gun, most of the other pigs scattered. A few turned toward the men, and were quickly brought down.

"Raina, are you hurt anywhere? You have blood on the edge of your pants." Kamon tried to keep his voice calm but knew he was far from succeeding. He helped ease her down from the tree limb, letting her slide the length of his body.

"I'm fine," Raina assured them, taking a deep breath of calm. "But there for a minute..., whew."

"Dang Raina, that blasted pig scared five years off my life," Liam complained as he hugged her. "That old sow must weigh four hundred pounds or so."

Each man took turns hugging her as if their touch confirmed to them that she really was safe and unharmed.

A silent Kamon pulled her back in his arms, closing his eyes to bring his body against hers. His dark golden skin was paler then usual, his breathing harsh and uneven. He pulled her tighter against his chest, his lips touching her forehead.

Raina looked up at him, eyes wide, questioning the unusual intimacy in front of the other men, but reveling in its possible meaning

The moment was not lost on the other men. Kamon never displayed affection toward Raina, or anyone else they had ever seen. His ability to step away from emotions was an oft discussed positive, and negative, attribute among those who knew him well. Until now.

"I need to say something to you, Raina."

As Deke and Trent turned to leave, Kamon added, "Please. I'd like all of you to stay. I want to say it in front of all of you who love Raina."

Staring directly at the four men, he declared in a low husky voice, "If I could choose my brothers, I would choose the four of you. As brothers, I want you all to know that I have loved Raina since she was small. I have tried to be as noble as I could and leave her alone. She deserves much more than I can ever be."

He paused, collecting his thoughts. "But I am only a man. And I am incomplete without her in my life. I'm walking around without a heart as she holds it in her hands. She makes me better than I could ever be without her. My very soul is connected to hers as it always has been and always will be. I know I am not worthy of her."

Raina lifted a hand to his face and started to speak. Kamon gently put his fingers over her mouth as he spoke directly to her.

"And now I can't do it anymore, Raina. You complete me, make me a whole being. I've always known that, and it scares the living hell out of me. I thought that meant that I was not whole by myself, that I was lacking somehow. That was my childhood talking."

Turning to the men he called brothers, he asked, "Do any of you have any objections to my taking our relationship further? Before you say anything, I want you to know that I would protect her with everything I am. No one could ever love her as much as I do."

Trent shared a look with the other men. "I think I speak for all of us. None of us have any objections. We love Raina and are proud to be called your brothers. Some things just are. It's damn obvious that its what you both want. As Catherine would say, the ancient ones are smiling. It's meant to be. Destiny."

"Hear, hear," agreed Deke, Sean and Liam, speaking simultaneous.

Kamon dropped to one knee, looking up to Raina's smiling face. "Raina Ramsey, will you marry me?"

Raina pulled Kamon up beside her. "Oh yeah!" she laughed happily. "Yes, yes, yes!"

"Tell Catherine to have a Priest at the Stone House in the morning" Kamon announced at he stared at Raina, a mix of possessiveness and desire in his eyes.

A beaming Raina raised a dark eyebrow, letting him see her feelings.

"Better yet, make that early afternoon," Kamon amended, his eyes never leaving Raina's face.

"You do know the Sgnoch Council is going to have a fit," grinned Sean gleefully. "They will want you two not to anticipate the marriage bed."

"Then they'll have a fit. And eventually get over it," Kamon announced.

EPILOGUE

"**K**amon is bringing Raina to the clinic for me to check her while I'm visiting. He says she isn't sick, but just doesn't feel well. He worries that she has some sort of virus," Brenna told Catherine as they sat in the waiting room of the small clinic building.

"You do know he's a mother hen where she concerned. She used to call Trent hover mother and danged if she didn't marry someone even more intense," laughed Catherine.

"True. But it's always easier to check her than to miss something vital. Besides, I love seeing them. They're the cutest couple ever."

"Agreed. Isn't it funny how their bonding worked out? Raina has become more intuitive and aware, but none of the mind transference which I would guess to be a throw-back brain anomaly. Kamon however, has done a one-eighty. He's mellowed and no longer shows any sign of pessimism. He's become much more like Raina than she has become like him," Catherine laughed at the irony of it. "Kamon will always be intense and mystical, that's just his nature, but personally I love the way he dotes on her."

"Maybe not a one eighty, more like a ninety-degree change. And he's truly happy. He told me last month that he has everything that he ever could have dreamed of, if he had been able to dream. Raina and a family. Ah, here they come. Holding hands, like newlyweds."

After hugs were exchanged between the three sisters and Kamon, Brenna said, "Okay Raina, I want you to just lay on the examining table, no tests yet. Now tell me again, exactly where you hurt."

"Brenna, I don't hurt. I just feel … off is the best way I can put it," Raina said frowning in thought. "Not normal, and no energy. I don't want to do anything. Not even try the new recipe that Alma just gave me. And since I've learned to cook, that's unusual as I love to make new stuff."

"You've become an excellent cook. But maybe you're doing too much," mused Catherine thoughtfully. "You've taken over at least half of the duties I had before Alexa and Gabe, even the business ones. You've restructured the Sgnoch Council so that every member has specific duties, but is cross-trained to fill in for anyone else."

"And she's implemented a morning play group for our twins and all the pre-school age kids in the valley," reminded Kamon, his eyes on his smiling wife.

"Hate to say it, but the nursery and pre-school were in self-defense. Russell and Robert need to be socialized, they could easily become spoiled brats. Since Alma MacPherson runs the program now, she includes anyone under five. Hooray!" Raina declared.

"That play group is one of the best things in the valley," Catherine declared. "Not only does it socialize our little ones but our elders also," she laughed. "Alma says that John McDougall and Duncan Frasier volunteer every day, but that most of the valley elders give a substantial amount of time to the school. The Anderson's grandfather visited from Edinburg and had so much fun that he's decided to relocate here. He's become part of team-grandparents. Its been a long time since we've had this many small children here at Shadow Valley."

Brenna laughed. "Oh yeah, Alma said that last week she had as many volunteers as she had children. She says it looks like a senior citizen's daycare. Both the elders and the little ones love it. And she thinks the whole idea is wonderful, Raina."

"Yep. Raina's wonderful," stated Kamon firmly, his warm gaze never leaving her face.

"Okay Kamon, I'm rolling my eyes now. Raina, hold very still now." Brenna placed her hands on Raina's arms and slowly moved her hands downward, over her head, then torso, then to the rest of her body. Catherine and Kamon watched as Brenna closed her eyes to examine her sister.

"Ah Brenna, your hands are so warm, they feel wonderful," murmured Raina, basking in the warmth and TLC. "I love your healing hands."

"That's the favorite thing in my examinations for most people, warm hands," chuckled Brenna. "How old are Russell and Robert now?" Brenna asked.

"They're a little over a year old as you fully know as you are a godparent." Raina's eyes widened as she put the question together with an answer. "No. no. I am not pregnant again. No. Dammit, Kamon stop grinning like a loon. Honestly if you don't stop grinning like an idiot, I'm going to be really mad."

Kamon's grin broadened even more, but he remained silent, his eyes shining.

"Brenna, I've used birth control religiously. I've never skipped a day. C'mon, am I really pregnant again? The twins are only a year old. We wanted a family while I was young, but dammit not now."

"Yep, you're pregnant," announced Brenna. "About six weeks. You know the drill. You have to slow down. Get lots of sleep, rest, eat right, etc. So you have to get more help for the twins. Now you want to know the gender?"

Raina held tightly to Kamon's hand. "Yes. No. Yes. Kamon, help me. I don't know."

"Sweetheart, we've talked about this. Before we married, we talked about this. Marriage is a compromise but since decisions have to be made, that decision is ultimately yours. Whatever is best for you is best for me. I mean that with all my heart and all my being. Forever. It's what you want. I'm okay with whatever you decide. Forevermore," he vowed, his dark eyes gentle and loving.

"Well, what I have decided is that I am not having a baby every year for the next 18 years. This pregnancy, but Brenna, there has got to be some kind of birth control that works for me and Kamon. A better one than the one we have," she clarified.

"Actually, there's a lot of possibilities; a Depo Provera shot every three months, snip-snip to Kamon, an IUD, a different pill, etc."

Kamon turned pale, sat straighter, grimaced as if in pain, then said, "Again, its whatever Raina wants. If it means snip-snip, then that's what I do. Forevermore," his gaze toward Raina was intimate.

"And sister-of-mine he spoils you rotten," stated Catherine. "He's a total hands-on Dad and he thinks you hung the moon."

"Don't forget the sun," Kamon laughed lightly. "I'm positive she hung that too, and maybe the stars. Shimmering sunshine is what she is in my life. And your husbands are as bad as I am. They're perfectly willing to give me advice on everything from candy gifts to diaper changing."

"Stop avoiding the issue," demanded Brenna. "Do you want to know the gender or no?"

"No," answered Raina. "This time I want it to be a surprise. Kamon? Okay with you?"

"Whatever you want, sweetheart. Wait or not," he shrugged his shoulders. "It doesn't matter as we will get whatever we get."

Turning to Brenna he asked in a serious voice, "What is wrong? I am not Mind Walking, but I feel that there's something else going on. A tension about you, Brenna. And that I do want to know. Whatever affects Raina is too important for me to not know. So is there anything wrong?"

"Raina?" asked Brenna.

"Whatever it is, I agree. Bad or good, Kamon and I are one, we always will be. We will handle it together."

"O-kay," Brenna agreed, biting her lip to keep her smile from being. "You're having another set of twins."

Instead of the expected gasp of horror, Raina burst out laughing. Pulling down Kamon for a hug, she says "Kamon never does anything half way. But really, Kamon. Four in two years? Is that some kind of record for Shadow Valley?" She asked Catherine her laughter still hanging in the air.

"I'm not sure about records, but twins do run in the Ramsey family as you well know. And congratulations," Catherine added, giving her youngest sister a long hug, then doing the same for Kamon.

"And Raina's health?" Kamon frowned. "There's nothing wrong? The babies are okay? We didn't plan this pregnancy, but she knows I'll do everything possible to make it as easy as it can be."

"Nothing's wrong. She and they are both in perfect health. Because they're twins, I'll see you in three weeks at the Spring Creek Clinic though. Just like before." Brenna added, "In case there's any kind of problem, Kamon, I know you will call me."

After they left, Catherine turned to Brenna and asked, "Okay what gives? If Raina and the babies are healthy, why are you giddy? You're almost bursting. And don't you even think about lying to me with medical hocus pocus."

"Ah, Catherine, we are so blessed! Raina and Kamon are going to have their hands full, and the entire valley will be involved. They have those Kamon look-alike twin boys, Russell and Robert. And now another set of twins."

Turning to Catherine, matriarchal leader and Seer of the tribal clan Ramsey, Brenna let the tears run freely down her face. "Raina and Kamon are having twin girls. Twin Gifted girls."

FIRST CHAPTER OF THE NEXT BOOK

RETURN TO SHADOW

Shadow Valley Series

CHAPTER ONE

Robert Morrison Neal stood across the driveway to get a better view of the large house he had spent three solid months of intense physical work helping to renovate.

Damn, it looked good.

The massive house had been built years before, but hadn't been lived in for a couple of years before he bought it. It was too isolated from neighbors for many people, even though it was just a few miles from the little town of Spring Creek, Arkansas. For other people, it was too much effort, or too costly to restore. The property came with a hundred acres of forest; mostly hickory, ash, and the massive white oak trees.

He had asked a cousin, Kamon Youngblood, to redesign the structure to modernize and upgrade everything to make it into a comfortable home. Kamon, a gifted architect, suggested a wider wooden porch to wrap around the front and the side of the two story structure, new windows and doors, and refinishing the wooden exterior. The exterior of the house was built from white oak tree, a hardwood native to the area. Kamon had also designed a dream kitchen with pecan cabinets, a huge island with seats, and shiny new appliances throughout. All other rooms in the large house had been modernized, even the apartment a former employee used extending off the kitchen.

When it was time for the interior decorating, Bob was in his own element as color was at the heart of his profession. He had chosen soft earth tones mingled with blues and greens throughout the house to give the huge, high ceiling rooms a warmer feeling. He had taken his collection of furniture out of storage, then bought complimentary pieces over the internet to furnish the home he meant to live in for a long time. He smiled as he reviewed his property. This home was for him. What he wanted and was comfortable with in this new life he had chosen.

Jennifer would have hated it. She liked the sleek modern style with lots of grays and blacks with sharp edges of light. And he had spoiled her unreservedly, giving her what she wanted. Anything. Everything. Whatever it took to make her happy. And it had almost robbed him of his soul when she died.

Shaking his head to clear the memories, he glanced toward the little house of his only employee, Hank Bond. One of the conditions to buy the property had been to keep the middle-aged man employed for a year. Since he was unsure of what this new venture in moving would require, he had readily agreed. A smart, unplanned move for which he was grateful.

Hank was a gem, knowing what had to be done, and doing it. He took care of the horses and did other general work around the place, even cooking some of the meals they shared as they became very good friends.

The barn was in good condition to stable the two horses that had come with the property. His plans were to buy a few more horses, ranch a little, and try to have a semi-normal life. Along with the horses, the property came with a mama barn cat, her newborn kittens, and a huge mongrel dog name Hugo.

Thinking of Hugo brought the realization that he heard a deep barking from around the bend of the road in front of the house. A panicked bark. If that clueless dog found another porcupine, he was going to … take him back to the vet, he admitted to himself. Maybe Hugo had found something harmless, he hoped, beginning to jog toward the alarmed barking sound.

Hugo sat on the side of the road in front of two small children who were standing protectively between Hugo and a huddled body on the ground. As Bob jogged up, the tiny girl stepped forward with her right hand holding a large stick.

"Don'cha come any closer," she demanded. "I'll hit you with this stick."

Bob glanced at the little boy with the distinctive features

of a Down Syndrome child, staring wide-eyed at him. Bob sat back on his heels beside Hugo to make himself the same height as the little girl.

"Hi, my name's Bob and that's Hugo," he said softly pointing to the dog. "What's yours?"

"My name's Elizabeth, but people call me Lizzie. That's Sammy," she pointed at the little boy. "And that's Mommy," she said, pointing to the unmoving woman laying on the ground. "Are you a bad man?" Lizzie asked narrowing her eyes. "Cause this stick can hurt you."

"No, I'm not. I'm a very good man," he said slowly. "It looks like your mommy may need some help though. I'm going check her so that I can see what she needs."

Kneeling, Bob gently lifted the edge of the ragged coat from the mother's shoulders, noting the bloodstained clothing. His breath caught in his throat as he saw the bloody, swollen face. "Easy, it's okay," he reassured the woman softly. "I'll call an ambulance ..." he started to say.

"Please, please no ambulance. He'll kill all of us." A small hand reached through the sleeve of the ragged coat to clasp his arm. "Promise no ambulance. Please, please," she begged, her voice breaking.

"Shh, shh. Its all right. Okay, no ambulance for right now. I'll call a friend to help you get to my house. My house is just around that bend in the road," he explained softly. He didn't know if she heard him or not as she slid into unconsciousness.

Quickly hitting speed dial, he said, "Deke, I need your help. It's an emergency. Bring Brenna. I found an injured woman and two small children at the bend of the road just before the house."

"We're on our way. We'll leave the kids here with Patty." The line went dead. Never one to ask questions in an emergency, Deke Paxton could be counted on during any crisis. And Brenna, a distant cousin of his, was a healer extraordinaire, the best physician anyone could know. Someone with very special skills.

"Some friends are coming to help carry your mom up to

my house," he carefully explained to Lizzy. "Deke's a good guy too. And his wife is coming, she's a doctor," he explained carefully. "They'll help your mommy."

"Ok," the little girl agreed slowly, laying the big stick on the ground. "Mommy does need help, she's hurt. And Sammy doesn't talk, and if you make fun of him, I'll beat you up," promised the little gingered-haired girl, her face fierce with determination.

"No one should make fun of other people," pronounced Bob firmly. "That's wrong and rude."

"Is 'rude' one of them words only adults can say? Cause it's mean too. Some people make fun of Sammy, and I want to hit them. And I'm not sorry."

Bob was unsure what to say next when Deke's large black truck slide to a stop near them.   Brenna immediately hurried from the truck carrying a small black bag. Kneeling beside the unconscious woman, she checked the woman's breathing then run her hands slowly over her ribcage. Closing her eyes, she carefully ran her hands over the rest of the body.

Looking up first at Deke, then at Bob, she murmured, "Her breathing is shallow, but that's because she may have bruised ribs, but no punctures. Her legs seem okay, but we'll have to use butterflies or stiches on some of the cuts. Her left arm is badly bruised, but I don't feel that it is broken. There's a lot of seeping wounds and dried blood. I think it's safe to move her, although it's easier on her before she wakes up. Deke, can you carry her in the truck? Keep her wrapped in the coverings she's in for now."

She turned to the children as Deke carefully lifted the woman and slid into the passenger side of the truck, holding the woman. "We're going to take good care of your mommy," she told the children. "Bob will walk with you to his house just around the bend," she instructed. She quickly got in the driver's seat and drove toward the house.

"Where's they taking mommy?" Lizzie demanded. "I wanta' go with her. She needs us." The little girl started to cry. Sammy looked at her, and tears formed in his eyes.

"Hey guys, it's okay. They're taking your mommy to my house so we can make her better. There's no room in the truck for us all, but my house is right around that bend," Bob pointed in the direction, hoping that would calm down the children for a minute. Taking each child by the hand, Bob walked as rapidly as he could toward the house, Hugo walking beside Sammy.

"What is that?" Lizzie asked, sniffing back tears, tugging him to a stop. "That building up there?"

Bob looked to see what she was asking. His house was the only thing in her sight. From where they were standing, the barn, outbuildings, and Hank's house couldn't be seen.

"Keep walking," Bob encouraged. "Lizzie, that's my house. That's where I live."

"Nope." Lizzie's voice was firm, no nonsense. "Nobody lives in a house that big. Do you live in a school or a store? I never ever saw a building that big."

Deciding that explanations would take time and energy, Bob decided to ignore the questions. "Hurry, let's get to where your mom is. Deke and Brenna may need our help."

Those seemed to be the magic words. The children moved so rapidly that they were almost running, Hugo loping alongside a fast shuffling Sammie.

Hugo bounded up the short stairs onto the porch, with the children right behind him. Bob opened the front door, and they all hurried into the living area.

Lizzie skidded to a stop, her mouth breathing in an "Oh" sound. "This is the biggest room in the world I bet'cha. Is that a fireplace?" Answering her own question, she said, "Yep, it's a fireplace cause its gots wood in there, and its built of rock. Why do you need two couches, and all them chairs and tables?"

Sammie glanced around, but was more interested in playing with Hugo. The dog had rolled over with his feet in the air.

"Hugo wants you to rub his tummy," Bob told the Sammy. When the little boy didn't respond, Bob took one of his tiny star-like hands and moved them over Hugo's tummy. The little boys small slant eyes sparkled as Hugo wiggled.

"Where's mommy?" Lizzie suddenly demanded, looking around for her.

"Brenna? Deke?" Bob called loudly.

"Here," came the muffled reply from one of the nearby downstairs bedrooms. "In here, Bob. And please bring the children. Their mother needs to see them for a moment."

Sammy jumped to his feet to shadow a running Lizzie, as she followed the sound of Deke's voice.

"Momma, oh momma," cried Lizzie, Sammy behind her.

"Easy sweetie, easy," Brenna reached out a hand to stop the children from flinging themselves on their mother's body. "Your mommy's hurt right now, but she wanted to see you, to be sure you're all right," Brenna gave a warm smile to each child.

"You're okay?" asked the woman softly, her one-eyed gaze on the children. "The dog didn't hurt you?"

"Oh no, mama. The dog's name is Hugo, he's big, but he likes to have his tummy rubbed. Sammy does that, huh, Sammy?" At Sammy's nod, she continued, "Momma, this house is bigger than a store. And the fireplace is so big I could stand up in it if I wanted." Then added, "But I don't want to."

Bob had to swallow hard as he stood just outside the room. The woman was an unrecognizable bloody mess. Her hair was matted with blood, stuck together in dirty tangles, one eye swollen completely shut, the other a mere slit of green. Her face was turning a blackish-purple color as was the arm that he could see. Several small cuts appeared to be red and puffy, but were no longer bleeding. The woman seemed to be struggling to stay awake, then with a tiny groan of pain, her eyes slowly closed, and she succumbed to deep sleep or unconsciousness.

Brenna spoke directly to the children. "Lizzie, Sammie, my name is Brenna. I'm a doctor, I take care of people who need care. That's my husband Deke over there," she indicated with a hand wave toward the large man at the back of the bedroom. "And you already know Bob. And I have little children too."

Brenna's eyes held sincerity as she added, "And we're going to help your momma. I need to check a couple of things still. And Bob, I may want to stay here tonight if that's all right with you, just to be sure that ..., that everything's okay".

Deke watched her for a moment as she looked from him, then back to the kids. The large man's eyes warmed with understanding, then replied to Brenna. "Well, while you're being sure, maybe we could raid the refrigerator and get some snacks to eat. Would you like to help me find stuff?" he asked the children.

"Sure. We like to eat snacks, whatever that is," Lizzie stated firmly, taking one of Deke's hands. Sammie took Lizzie's other one. "We'll be back," she told her mother as they walked out.

Moving to the doorway out of Leeann's hearing range, Brenna lowered her voice.

"Bob, her name is Leeann Downey. We've had very little time to talk as she's in a lot of pain, but she says she's fleeing an abusive husband. I've taken pictures just in case she needs them later. She has multiple cuts and bruises. Her arm was dislocated, and her back is still bleeding, that's why she is turned on her side. She didn't want the children to see the bandages covering the lacerations. He beat her with his belt, the buckle, and his fists."

She took a deep breath, "There's also old scars where he must have taken his belt to her back and legs. The indications are that this is not the first time, nor the tenth time he's beat her. You need to know all this as several decisions have to be made. She has sixty-seven dollars and twenty-five cents that she's been able to save over the last two years and no other resources."

Brenna watched Leeann's face as she continued to talk in a low murmur. "She says her husband drinks, and uses opioids mixed with meth. She doesn't know what else. I have given her my promise that I will not take her to a hospital. With the pain and sleeping medications I've given her, she's probably out until the morning, when she can be moved. Then I'll take her and the children home with me for awhile. Deke won't mind."

"Brenna, I know you're working this week for Dr. Farrison. That means that your helper, Patty, and Deke, would be caring for her, and her children, plus your two. You're not going to be as available as I am. Why would you move her from here?"

Brenna held his gaze for a full minute, saying nothing.

Bob shook his head slightly. "I can handle whatever it is. She and the children can stay here," he said firmly. "Brenna, there's certainly enough room here, and I can change bandages as you know." A fleeting look of sorrow crossed his face, then he stood up straighter.

"Bob, are you sure? It's a big undertaking. I can stay tonight and check in tomorrow night but ...."

"I'm positive," he asserted, falling silent, letting Brenna decide, as she was one of the handful of people who knew his background.

Brenna nibbled on her lower lip in thought as she studied Bob for several moments. "Okay, here's what would work best. There's a retired nurse that I think would be willing to take on short-term nursing duties for a week or so. She's done it several times for me before. She's confidential and motherly. One of the things that this asshole did to Leeann was to also beat her around the pelvic area with his fists and belt. Quit frankly, I think Leeann would be more comfortable with a female nurse doing those duties that some of this is going to require."

"Damn, I liked to get my hands on that Son of ...."

"You'd have to stand in line," Brenna interrupted. "And you would have to hurry before Deke and I got there. But remember, it's only a matter of time until this abusive husband finds out where she is. He'll want her back to take out his anger on. The longer that time is the better, so the less people that know where she is, the more time she has to heal. We can help her deal with some decisions she'll have to make in the future. For now, getting her healed is the goal. Also for now, having full charge of two small, very active children will be more than enough for you to worry about. Lizzie seems to be pretty self-confident," Brenna grinned.

"Ya think?" Bob kidded. "She's threated me with a stick if I hurt her mother, or was mean to Sammie. I have to admit I like that kid's style."

"Leeann said she was four and a half, and Sammie is seven-years-old. Lizzie's more like four going on forty-four," chuckled Brenna, pushing her long auburn braid to her back. "Catherine's Alexa is about the same age. Let's not arrange a play-date for them – they might take over this part of the state of Arkansas. Our three-year-old son, Brandon, follows Alexa around and just does whatever she tells him to do. She rewards him with cookies. Smart boy," she grinned.

Turning serious, she asked, "Leeann thinks she's leaving here tomorrow, but she won't even be able to get out of bed by then. Besides her pelvic area, her back and left arm are a mass of bruises and cuts when he used the buckle end of his belt on her. And," she added, "she doesn't know how long she was unconscious. Except for her eye, there's no other serious head injuries, although she does have a very mild concussion which is going to require some time to heal."

"How long are you talking about Brenna. For her to heal? Any idea?"

"Three or four days in bed, then rest for several more with frequent naps. Good food, lots of sleep with no activity." She narrowed her grass-green eyes in thought. "And no emotional stress. And don't ask because I don't know how in the hell we're going to manage that. She's sound asleep, lets check the children."

Bob walked into his kitchen behind Brenna. Seated at the breakfast bar was Deke, Lizzie and Sammie with plates of bacon, eggs, and toast in front of each of them. Hank was at the stove with his back to them.

Glancing up, Hank asked. "You all want me to fry up some more eggs or bacon? It won't take but just a minute."

"We're good for now," Deke answered, his eyes focused on Brenna.

Lizzie turned around on her stool when she heard them enter. "Mr. Bob, this is one of those rest-er-runt kitchens I saw in a magazine at the general store once." She pointed to where a grinning Hank stood over the stove with a spatula in his hand. "Mr. Hank says we're having breakfast for dinner, and that we can eat all we want. Can we?" she asked hesitantly.

"Sure," Bob answered. "I love to see people eat. Hey, Hank. Thanks for coming up to help."

"Deke and Lizzie filled me in on some stuff." His smile was grim as he added, "Maybe we can take some gas down the road and get the truck out of the driveway. Lizzie said they run out of gas."

"Lizzie, Sammie," Brenna focused her attention on the children. "Your mommy needs to rest for a few days so she can get better. You're going to stay here with her. Bob and Hank live here, and Deke and I live next door." She didn't tell them that next door was several hundred acres over. "When you finish your snack, I'm going to get you washed up and let you sleep in a room next to your momma."

"I want to sleep with momma," Lizzie whined. Sammie blinked at Lizzie, then screwed up his face to cry too.

Brenna hastily assured them, "Momma hurts right now and needs to sleep by herself. I'm going to rest in a recliner by her bed to be sure she is okay tonight. I'll leave the door open and the light on so you can see us. What did you leave in your truck?" She asked, looking to distract them and to gain information.

"We left momma's quilts that she made. We were wrapped up in them 'cause the truck don't got no heater momma said. And it was cold."

"Nothing else?" asked Brenna. "No clothes, or toys?"

"Nope," Lizzie said matter-of-factly. "We had to hurry and leave before he comed back. We had rag dollies mama made, but he burned them last winter."

The adults shared a quick incredulous look.

"There's some t-shirts in the top drawer in the bedroom, if you want to use them," Bob stated. "They might make night shirts. Brenna, you know you can have anything that I have. Oh, except Hugo. We're going to keep him here," he smiled at the children, including them in the decision.

"Yep. We're gonna keep him here," echoed Lizzie. Hugo lay beside the table, probably hoping for dropped tidbits.

"While you put gas in the truck, I'll get Lizzie and Sammie washed up and into bed. Then I need to call Mrs. Hansen," Brenna declared, putting a hand on Lizzie's shoulder to move her toward the bedroom. "Bob, would you share our conversation with Deke and Hank, please?"